HODDER HOUSE

A Novella

Ash Ericmore

Written by: Ash Ericmore

Copyright © 2021 Ash Ericmore

All Rights Reserved. This is a work of fiction. No part of this publication may be reproduced, distributed, or transmitted in any form or by any means, except in the case of brief quotations embodied in critical reviews.

ISBN: 9798354123605

CHAPTER 1

Sophie squinted through the rain. Jesus wept. *In three hundred metres turn right.* The GPS shook her. Fucking hell. She hated driving in the dark. That was bad enough. But driving in the dark … in the rain. She just wasn't used to it. And she'd had to drive halfway across the country. And she was running a little late.

And she really didn't want to be late for this.

Her phone—currently on a holder stuck to the windscreen and acting as GPS—chimed *again*, and the small half notification came up.

Where are you? You're going …

Then it cut off. The notification promptly disappeared. That was about the twelfth. She reach forward to prod the screen. It wouldn't hurt. Not this once. She had to know what they were saying in the chat. The car drifted as her hand and her eyes focussed on the phone. A horn from a car on the other side of the road. Her attention drawn back to her driving, and that slight push of shit trying to escape her at the sound, and she righted the vehicle. "Or perhaps not," she muttered to herself. Quick squint at the screen. She was only a couple of miles out. She could wait.

Another chime.

A quick look. Don't focus. She saw it was another message from the private group that had been created just for tonight. But she didn't read it. It was best not to look, maybe not cause a head-on with something else going the other way. Not for the sake of ten minutes.

She realised she was shaking. Just a little. A buzz. She was excited. Of course she was excited. This was the pinnacle of the calendar this year. Well, *her* calendar, anyway. Not that she had much of a calendar. Not since Damon had fucked off—and by fucked off, she meant *been fucked off*. They'd met in a bar about two wasted years ago. Hit it off. He didn't seem like the other fuck boys at the place. He was interesting. He shared her opinions. *He had opinions*. And then they'd found out that they had a shared love. *Horror*. It was exciting at first, sharing films, cuddling up on the sofa. Popcorn. Netflix. Chill.

Turned out he was a dick.

But that was another story. Either way, without him she'd have never found The Horror Tribe Podcast. Well, she might have. Anyway. That was what tonight was all about. Meeting the other Patreon supporters. The others from the same tier that she was. With all this extra cash she had on hand from working at the insurance brokers—she was only an administrator, so it's not like it was real big money or anything—and being single, she'd only just two months ago moved from one tier to the next. She still didn't really understand Patreon, but fuck it. Two months back she to listen to the podcast a week early. She got to talk online with the hosts, too. Mike and Will. Behind the scenes stuff. In a chat room with the others. She felt like a real celebrity hunter. All for five pounds a month. But then she'd up'd. Taken a big leap too. Onto bigger things. For one hundred pounds a month she could would get to talk the hosts in a private room. Just the three of them. It was online, so nothing weird, but she could spend actual time with them. Will sounded pretty hot. You know. In all fairness, there was a little of that. *But that wasn't the point.* She'd get a t-shirt, films, and a few other things through the post. And once a quarter she'd be entered into the draw to visit one of their events. That was the main reason to up the outlay, really. There was one coming up, and she wanted in.

And she'd been picked.

Normally the event would involve five or six of the one hundred pound tier being chosen, and they would attend a special event laid on by the podcast. Sometimes it was a film screening, sometimes a meal out. Always good. Always horror themed. Those that had been were sworn to secrecy about it—and you could never get picked twice. From what she'd gathered, most of the one hundred pound Patreon supporters dropped down a level after they'd been chosen. Made sense she supposed.

But she might stay there for a while. Chat with Will some more. You never know.

So, she didn't know what she was going to. She had—under the strictest of secrecy—been provided with a postcode for a GPS and told when to arrive. That was it. Looking at the GPS when she'd plugged in the postcode, it looked like a small cul-de-sac in the middle of nowhere.

And she was just turning into the road now.

Intriguing.

CHAPTER 2

The house loomed at the end of the road. It was a narrow road, no other houses apart from the one at the end, with a turning circle. There were other cars parked in the turning circle. She hated it when people parked inside a turning circle. She pulled up behind the last one and parked there too. Fuck it. Sophie grabbed her phone from the holder and grabbed her bag, got out of the car. There were four people standing at the gates to the house already. Owners of the other cars no doubt. She tried to stay casual. Stroll over. Inside she was burning up with excitement. Looking forward to meeting the hosts. Will. Okay, Will. She was looking forward to meeting Will. She couldn't see him there. Just other supporters, perhaps. Sophie rolled her bag over her shoulder. Not a handbag. She was too cool for that. More a leather shoulder backpack thing. She'd found it in a charity shop. Loved it.

Of the four of them, there were two and two, men and women. One of the guys had been watching her since she pulled up. As she got closer, she could see a look of disappointment in his face. Hidden, but it was there. Probably thought she was the hosts. He brightened as she got closer. "Sophie's Choice?" he called. That drew the attention of the other three to her. They were all standing with their phones in their hands.

Sophie's Choice was her handle for Horror Tribe.

She grinned at the guy—hoped she didn't look too deranged—"Just Sophie is fine." She stuck out her hand and he took it, shaking it. Wasn't a strong handshake. A three second judgement on the guy—he was tall, thin, bearded, hipstery in the face, pebble glasses, red zip up hoodie, foppish, lanky, weak, pipe-legged trousers—told her that he probably wasn't going to become her new bff. He must have known her name because she was the last to arrive. "So who have we got?"

"I'm Lawrence, *Cable Guy* …" he added his username on the end, "… Maria, *Maria's That* …" he pointed at the first of the women. "David, *David Twelve* …" then the other guy. "And Tracy, *I'd Fuck Freddy in a Flash*." When he said her username, he glanced back to Sophie and raised his eyebrows. Had *that* look. Judgemental.

Sophie looked around the group, made quick guesses about them. Maria looked like she might be cool. Mid twenties. Smart, sophisticated, maybe. Not too weird. David looked like a nerd. And Tracy was, dressed in black. Slutty black. Looked like she was about eighteen and was here to party. Whatever. What did she really care about the others in the group? She just wanted to see what they were getting into. And meet Will. She looked by Larry. "Why are we waiting out here?"

Larry nodded to Maria. "Maria got here first, got a *Whatsapp* in the chat to wait for further information and to pass it along. So here we wait."

Sophie nodded slowly and looked up at the

house. Big. Gothic looking. Looked like one of those houses that ends up as a stock photo on the front of a hundred cheap horror books. Big set of doors at the front. Couple of windows on each side. Same upstairs. Big looking vee shape at the top. On the roof. Whatever that was called. Apex. Something. The garden was unkempt. Overgrown. The only thing keeping them on the path was a wooden fence. Little thing. Quaint, if it hadn't been left to rot. It looked like she could probably level the whole thing with a single kick.

She realised it was still raining.

Hadn't thought about it since she got out the car.

She looked around, hoping to see another car approach. Fucking hell. Where were they? Haunted house? Could be. Wasn't going to be a film showing, she guessed. The house was big enough for one, but with only five of them chosen this time, it seemed unlikely. There would be bedrooms in there, though. She smiled to herself. Cheeky. *He might be married.* You never know.

Suddenly there was a cluster of chimes and rings, and each of the five of their phones started ringing in tandem. Sophie pulled hers from her pocket. She recognised the ring. What's App, group video call. Fuck. What did that mean? She opened the app. Will grinning at her.

At everybody, she supposed.

"I'm guessing that you are all wondering why I gathered you here today?" He laughed. "No seriously.

Now you've all arrived, we should clear this up. Ah. I see the look of confusion as to how I know you're all there already." He winked into the camera and Sophie assumed it was for her, specifically. She flushed red. Stupid. "If you'd all like to line up at the fence and face the house." He waited while they did. "You can see if you look up—into the rain—I can see that too—there are several cameras mounted on the trees in the front garden and on the outside of the house." He paused for a second. "Actually, most of them won't be that clear in the rain. But trust me, they're there.

"Anyhow. We're going to be recording once you step over the threshold into the garden. What we have here, my favourite one hundreders is what is supposed to be the most haunted house in the country." He paused possibly for effect. "Never heard of it? Well, there's a reason for that. All will become clear in time.

"Once you enter the garden the game will commence. We're challenging you to spend the night in here. Me and Mike are in the studio watching and recording. You might hear from us every now and again—and the whole thing is being recorded. In the house there are cameras covering every inch of the floor. I would say recording for posterity, but it's a pre-recording for distribution. So just like always, you're going to be on air somewhere. So no hanky-panky." He laughed. "I'm looking at you, David."

Sophie shot a looked to David. Looked like a cherry tomato.

"Anyway. You are free to enter. We'll be recording everything. Hopefully you might see a ghost in there. Now put your phones away. I won't be in touch." He started mu-ha-ha-ing and killed the call.

Sophie looked at the house. Then at the other four. Everyone looked a little confused. They'd seen the recordings of a couple of these nights in the past. They were released to the other Patreon tiers after a couple of weeks. Will was always there. She frowned. Fucking rip off. And she was kind of expecting a little bit of royalty treatment. Some nice booze maybe. A film. A fucking kebab even. Not to be locked in a *haunted house*—that no one had ever heard of—for the night with dumb, dumber, slutty, and—she looked at … what was her name … Maria?—disappointment. Well. She supposed they should get on with it.

CHAPTER 3

Sophie went to the gate and pushed it open. "Everyone ready?"

There was an apathetic grumble from Maria. Tracy looked thoroughly enthralled by the prospect, and Lawrence looked like he was just happy to be locked in the house with the women. David? David just looked down. He was obviously going to be the shy boy. She smiled. "Come on Davey. Last one in's a wet fish." She might as well enjoy it.

She stepped into the garden. No turning back now. Her phone went into her pocket, and she turned, walking backwards down the path towards the front door. The others were following slowly. Apprehension in some cases. Politeness in others. It looked like David was taking up the rear. Very gentlemanly. Once in, he followed and closed the gate, the five of them approached the house. Up closer, Sophie could see it was red brick. Old windows. Wooden frames. There were steps up to the door. One of those semi-circle arched windows above it. Frosted. The front door was red. Wooden. In good repair. It looked like someone actually looked after the place. "Do we knock?" Sophie asked quietly, to no one in particular. Larry leaned across her to the handle of the front door. She slipped back slightly so he didn't touch her. He was *too* close.

He gripped the handle. Twisted. The door opened. Silently. "Knock," he said. "And the door will open."

The door swung inwards, and Sophie didn't get the haunted house creek that she was expecting. Very disappointing. Beyond was the hallway. Lights on. She stepped in. Looking around carefully. Part of her didn't believe in haunted houses, so this was no problem. Part of her expected there to be childish traps set up to scare them like a carnival house. Part of her was just disappointed.

There was a small part of her—so very small—that wanted the place to actually be haunted. For the shits and giggles. See a real ghost. Put it online. Have the piss ripped out of her. The accusations that it was made with Adobe Aftereffects. But she'd know it was real.

But let's be honest. None of that was going to happen.

Probably nothing. But that wouldn't make a good video, now would it? The boys must have something up their sleeves. "Knock, knock," she called into the house. The sound reverberated back to her.

"Come on, it's wet out here."

Sophie didn't know which of the women said it. Fucker. She stepped in and freed up the door to let the others in. She ignored the cooing they were making. She'd make her own judgement on the house and its authenticity. She looked around the ceiling. Cameras. They looked expensive, too. Little red lights flashing on the sides of them. Recording. The rest of the hallway was standard—what she'd call—*lavish*.

White marbled floor. White walls with a fancy dado rail. Flock wallpaper. There was a table in the middle of the room. Two doors on the left, two on the right. A stairwell going up the centre. It looked like something out of a film from the nineteen twenties. She glanced at the others. They were all doing much the same as her. Looking around. Gawking. She shook her head and strode to the table. There was a vase in the middle of it. Flowers. Pretty. She reached forward and touched them. They felt like they were made of plastic. But in water. It completed the illusion. There was a newspaper folded on the table. Like it had been delivered that morning, placed there by a butler. This was the sort of house that would have a butler. She picked it up. The date at the top of the page. 12th November, 1972. Sophie glanced down the page. The headline read, *Four disappear*. There was a picture of the house. This house. Prop. Had to be. She looked down the article enough to know that it was about this house and that the four occupants had mysteriously vanished on the night of 11th November. She tossed it back to the table.

"What is it?" Lawrence.

"Nothing. Just something to raise a few scares." She turned around, away from him. The others were all still between her and the door like she'd been nominated as some sort of leader. Well. She was on camera. Make the best of it. She looked back, over everybody. "Is someone going to shut that?" she motioned to the front door, left open. The rain pounding outside, the cold air coming through.

David—still taking up the rear—closed it

obediently.

Sophie pulled out her phone. It was six-thirty. She had to spend the night with this bunch, and be on camera the whole time. Well. She hadn't eaten since lunch time, half expecting there to be some sort of buffet. "Kitchen," she announced. There were other things that should have been investigated in the room. There was a telephone on a small square table. The phone looked like it was pre-war. Probably wouldn't have worked these days, even if it wasn't a prop. Which it probably was. She walked over to the first door on the left. Opening it into a library. Sophie felt off. There was something *wrong*. Something *felt* wrong. She glanced around. Very red. A lot of books. The whole room looked like a set from a posh black and white film. All sparkling new. She pulled the door shut. But it wasn't the kitchen. She turned and the whole group was watching her expectantly. She stared back at them. "What?" she whispered.

Then they all seemed to look the other way at the same time.

Jeez.

Sophie went to the next door. Second on the left. It was down the side of the beginning of the staircase. She opened it into the kitchen. "Ah," she said. That drew the attention of the others back to her. She shook her head and looked at them. "Kitchen," she said. "I'm starving." There seemed to be some murmur of agreement among the group, and then a mass following.

She went into the kitchen. Relatively old looking.

Big cooker. Large oak farmhouse table in the centre of the room. Five chairs around it. Will really wasn't coming, was he? She sighed and went to the fridge. Full of food. A bounty.

At least they were being looked after.

There was beer in the door. Real ales. Decent ones. Sophie took one and stuffed it up under her arm. Then she pulled a plate of sandwiches out. Poked them to see what was in there. Ham salad. Good enough for her. She had simple tastes. She took the beer and the sandwiches to the table and slid them both down, pulled the chair at the head out and sat. Lawrence followed her around the kitchen, to the fridge. Started rummaging inside. Sophie took a bite from the sandwich.

Fucking hell.

Good ham.

It was the most important part of the sandwich, in her opinion. Although it could be argued that the bread was, but that was pretty decent too. No complaints. A bottle opener was dropped onto the table next her. Made her jump. Nearly choked on her sandwich. She looked around. Tracy flashed a smile at her. And then took the seat next to her. She had a plate of chicken wings. A bottle of wine. Red. She screwed the lid off and poured herself a glass.

"I didn't see that in there," Sophie said.

Tracy looked at her like she was something she'd stepped in. Shrugged.

Sophie looked back to her own plate. It wasn't

like she'd asked for any. Fuck. She stuffed another bite into her mouth. Larry took the seat to the other side of her. Sausage rolls. She hadn't seen them either. Probably would have nabbed one for her plate. He was drinking European lager. Maria—plate of something fishy. Urg. Sophie didn't want to know what. And a shot of something. David had crisps. And milkshake. Huh.

CHAPTER 4

They finished eating in near silence. The only thing uttered was that prawns were Maria's favourite. Sophie took her phone out of her bag and slid it onto the table. It was seven now. "Now what?" she said. May as well get somebody else's input before she decided how to waste the rest of the evening.

It wasn't like she was going to get any action. She glanced at David. He wasn't old enough. And then Larry. *Just no*.

"We should explore," Larry said.

Sophie was thinking more about finding a bedroom and laying claim to it, before she ended up sleeping on the sofa, or worse, sharing. She glanced to Tracy. Uh.

"Find a ghost," he continued.

A ghost. He didn't really believe in such things did he? Christ. They were film fans. Books. Graphic novels. It's not like The Lost Boys actually existed.

"Let's," replied Maria.

Fucking hell. What was this, The Famous Five? There was a sudden shuffle of chairs and everyone except Sophie was standing. Apparently there had been a shift in power since the *choose what door to open* round had played out, and now Larry was calling the shots. Good, she thought to herself. Now she could do what she wanted without having to look over her shoulder.

Sophie suddenly realised that everyone was staring at her. She took another swig of beer. Met their looks with the same expectant look as them.

"Are you coming?" Larry said.

"Oh." Sophie smiled at him. More a grin really. "No. You go ahead. I'm just going to finish up here."

Larry shrugged, but she could see a little disappointment in his eyes. It was probably because he thought they should all stay together, but it could equally be that he was lusting after her and wanted to get her alone. She smiled inwardly. She would eat that nerd alive. A quick glance to David. Or that one. She shook her head. What the fuck? What was she thinking? She watched the four of them leave, back out through the door they'd come in. Sophie turned and looked around the empty room. She felt a little more comfortable now. Beer in hand. There was a pantry behind her. The rest of the kitchen was done out in an old farmhouse style. She looked at the table. They'd all left their plates and empty drinks behind. Well. She wasn't cleaning them up.

She got up. Left her plate on the table, but took her unfinished beer. Opened the door of the pantry. It was big enough to walk in. Stone walled. Probably to keep it cool. And cool it was. Even before she stepped in, the cold air brushed against the skin of her face. Sent a chill down her spine. Hairs on her arm raised. The room was dark. No window. About the size of a box bedroom. The walls, covered in shelves, were all empty. The pantry was bare. She looked at the floor before she stepped in. That was tiled. Like parquet, but not wood. In the room, the cold enveloped her. Surrounded her. She could feel the temperature of her body drop, just slightly. Another shiver.

She looked around quickly, and then stepped back out. Closed the door. Haunted or not, that room was chilling. Damn. Should have said it out loud. For the cameras. "Haunted or not," she said, in a presenting voice, "that room was chilling."

Now she'd said it out loud it sounded stupid.

Fucking hell.

Whatever. She walked across the kitchen to the door out into the hallway, and followed where the others had gone.

She looked at the table. Something was different. The paper. The paper was gone. One of them must have taken it. She wanted to smoke. Not a cigarette. Those things were gross. No. A joint. She hadn't had one in a couple of days. She would have brought some with her tonight, but, well, the cameras. Sophie stopped and listened.

She couldn't hear the others.

Probably fucked off upstairs to try and claim the bedrooms. Fuck. She should have gone with them. Gotten a bedroom with an en-suite.

CHAPTER 5

Sophie went over to the first door on the other side of the hallway. Pushed it open. It was the living room. She stepped in. Her shoes stopped making the clack of heels on tile, and it changed to carpet.

The room immediately felt warmer.

She pushed the door behind her so that it was *almost* closed. Not latched. She just wanted a little privacy. The room invited her inside. There was a roaring fire, crackling and spitting with logs glowing red. She looked up to the camera in the corner, the ceiling. She raised a toast, knowing that Will was watching. Showing her pleasure at the room. There was a thick, heavy, rug in front of the fire, just close enough that it would be perfect for fucking on. Shame. A couple of wingback chairs, a chaise lounge. She went to one of the chairs that faced the fire and placed her drink down on the small round table that was between it and the other chair. Sat. She stared into the fire.

Haunted, she thought. *Yeah*. It felt more like a ski lodge.

She smiled to herself and let herself warm in the radiance of the flames, perfect after the food. Her eyelids felt heavy. The drive was long and difficult in the rain. Especially after it had gotten dark. She closed her eyes. Listened to the hypnotic call of the fireplace. She could hear the occasional creak from the floor above her. It was the others. Moving about. Arguing over who gets the best room. It wasn't going to be her. She was happy there, for now. Take what was left over. Whatever. She opened her eyes, and picked the drink back up, taking a swig. She didn't really want to go to sleep, to be honest.

Another creak from above.

Sophie pushed herself out of the chair. She really should go and see what they were doing upstairs. After all, falling asleep in the chair wasn't exactly scintillating watching, now was it?

She went to the door and pulled it open. The hallway felt cold after she'd been so toasty in the living room. Damn it. *Better find a bed*, she supposed. Sophie took a final swig from the beer bottle and placed it down on the table in place of the gone newspaper, and headed over to the stairs. She stopped. She didn't have a change of clothes or anything. Wasn't told to bring any. Just her bag. She shrugged it off. Oh well. One night won't hurt, will it? She put one foot in front of the other on the stairs. The drink must have hit her hard, she felt a little light headed. She held onto the bannister and made her way up. Straight at first, the stairwell curved around to the right, before joining the landing at the top. By the time she got there she felt quite tired. Probably the mixture of the beer and the fire. The long drive. But she shook it off. Pulled her phone from her pocket. Ten o'clock. She stared at the numbers. It was only seven a few minutes ago. She looked down the hallway on the landing. There were six doors, three on each side, and the hall ended with a window.

Bedrooms, she assumed. Bathrooms. One door was open and the others all closed. She frowned and looked at her phone again. Maybe she'd fallen asleep in the living room. She shook the phone like that might help and looked at the time again. Unsurprisingly, it was still the same.

Shit.

She'd slept half the evening. She looked down the corridor. And they'd all done whatever they'd done and had turned in. Leaving her asleep downstairs. Fuck it. She was probably going to be in trouble with Will and Mike for fucking up their show. Hopefully the others had done better. *Seen a ghost* or some shit. She pushed the phone in her pocket and went to the only open door in the hallway.

Carefully looked inside to make sure it was vacant.

It was dark, but she could see there was nobody in the bed. Pushing the door open, she fumbled around and found the light switch on the wall. Flicked it on. The room lit up. It was … surprisingly nice. She pushed it closed. Latched it. There was a bed. Big double. Probably king or something. A chest at the base of it. Looked like a treasure chest. Old. Antique. A wardrobe. Also old. There was a second door on the far side of the room. She crossed, letting her fingers drift along the wood of the front of the wardrobe, and dropped her bag on the end of the bed. She opened the second door. Bathroom. En-suite. Maybe they all had bathrooms attached? Maybe the others had left her the best room. Doubt. Still, she had it, and that was what mattered. She sat on the edge of the bed. Soft, but not too soft. Perfect. Just how she liked it. Sophie kicked her shoes off, and wiggled her toes. Free at last. She went to the wardrobe. Inside hung some clothes. A red dress. Looked like a period dress. Something *extremely* expensive. A set of under garments that certainly weren't period. Looked like chic-slut. She pulled them out and admired them. Nice. Her size too. She placed them back in. Looked at the dress. Also her size. Odd. She flipped through the other hangers. All garments in her size. Perfect fit. All her style. And all sexy as hell.

She pushed the wardrobe closed. Kinda wanted to put on the red dress. See what it looked like, but that also felt a bit weird. She stopped, looked into the corner of the room. Camera. Flashing red light. Yeah. She was being watched, too.

CHAPTER 6

Sophie opened the door of the en-suite and stepped in. She looked around the ceiling. Camera-less. Good. She pushed the door closed, shutting the bedroom out. The bathroom had one of those freestanding tubs. One with four legs and gold taps. Classy. A walk in shower. Toilet. Sink. It stood apart from the rest of the house. It was all modern. Perfectly so. She went to the tub and ran her fingers along the cool rim. She was bathing. Guaranteed. The question was now, or in the morning?

The thought had crossed her mind that this whole experience was a set up and that the instant she was in bed with the lights out—meaning that *all* the participants were in bed—all hell would break loose and the show would start.

Perhaps she should let that happen, if it was going to? She didn't want to piss anyone off more than she had done already, by falling asleep downstairs. She turned back to the door. Sighed.

Probably.

Sophie went back into the bedroom and over to the bed. She lifted her bag onto the floor and stripped out of the top layer of her clothes. Down to a t-shirt— that she knew covered her below the panty-line. Kept her undies on, obviously. Kind of wanted to give the boys a show, but not show too much. Right? She was also aware that anything she did show could—

would—be online somewhere, so not matter what, she wasn't about to get naked. She slid into the bed. Wasn't tired now. Maybe turn the light off for half an hour and see what happened. Maybe go and have a bath then? She set her phone on the night table and flipped the lights off.

Sophie lay in the dark, staring at the ceiling. There was the shadow of the light fitting in the middle of it, extending out, spidering across the artex. Fucking artex—

Not tired.

Shit.

She turned and faced the other way. Now all she could see was the red light of the peep show flashing on and off. Probably had night vision. Anyway. She wondered how long it was going to be before they got this show on the road, so to speak. Hm. Now she kinda wanted a snack. She was sure there was one of those Weight Watchers salted caramel things in her bag. She wasn't *that* snacky. Those things looked great. *Fluffy centres, my arse*. They were like chewing on a condom. Her eyes lowered, down the wall, and to the door. She could see the light of the hallway beyond, under the crack at the bottom.

A shadow.

Something moved out there.

It was probably one of the boys going for a piss.

For fuck's sake. They'd never get this thing started if these people didn't go to bed and stay there. She watched the shadow. It glided across the light at the bottom of the door and stopped. Whoever it was, standing on the other side of the door. Fucking hell. One of them was going to try it on. *On camera.* Not a fucking chance.

She watched, and waited, taking silent bets in her head. Was it the hipster, or the boy? Wasn't high odds on it being the boy. Way too shy. What chance Larry thought he had with her was another matter. Stupid sausage roll muncher. She watched as the handle on the door moved. Just an inch. The cheek of it. Fucker thought he was going to get some.

Then the thought crossed her mind that it mind not be Larry. What if it was Maria? Tracy? Huh. Well, traditionally she didn't swing that way, and while the idea may pique her interest at some other point in the future … not while she was on fucking camera. What the fuck were they thinking?

By this point, Sophie's heart rate had raised and she was in quite the fluster. She wanted to roll over and turn the light on. End it. Whoever it was would turn away. Scurry from the door. And she'd never know who it was. But there was a nagging part of her that wanted to wait until the door was open and then flip the light on. Catch them red handed. If it was Maria, well, arrangements could be made for another night. Maybe. She waited. Breath held.

The door handle moved again. The latch clicked free, and the door opened a couple of inches.

Sophie rolled over and flipped the light on. The room illuminated. She turned back in the bed and sat up. Looked straight at them.

And smiled.

CHAPTER 7

Even though he was standing with the light from the hall behind him, the light from the lamp was enough, she could tell it was Will. Where he had come from she both didn't know, and to be honest, didn't care. He had his arm up against the frame, above his head, leaning. Whether he was trying to look cool or not, she had no idea. Again. Didn't care. She sat back, a small smile. She knew he'd be able to see her face clearly, with the extra light behind him. The lamp on her face.

So, the game was about to begin. She knew it. As soon as the lights were out. She could write the script for these things.

Will stepped into the room and pushed the door closed behind him, cutting the extra light from the hallway out. Then she could see him properly. Had a cheeky half smile. She pushed the covers back and got to the edge of the bed. Getting up. "So, what's happening?" she asked.

"Whoa, whoa," he replied. He waved his hands downwards, signifying that she shouldn't be in such a hurry.

She couldn't help it. She complied without word. It was Will. Of course she did. He walked across the room to her, and stood over her. It sent a tingle down her spine. She was well aware of her half-nakedness. "What are you doing here? I thought you were in the studio."

"That was for everybody else's benefit."

Was she going to be part of the show? Like properly? She turned and looked to the corner of the room. "The camera," she said. "It's recording. People will see."

Will pulled something out of his pocket. A remote. He pushed the button on it and the red light of the camera extinguished. "Now we're alone," he said, quietly.

"What's the prank?" she asked, sitting forward. Finally. Something to do that was going to be worth the trip. Get one over on the other four. A stooge for the show. "What do you want me to do?"

"Nothing," he breathed. "Just lay back." He pulled on his belt, loosening it.

"What?" Sophie's eyes widened. "What do you mean?" She instinctively pushed herself back on the bed, towards the headboard.

Will stopped. Belt half undone. "Do you want me to stop?"

"No," she said quickly. *Fuck no.* She glanced at the camera again, just to be sure. It was still off.

Will saw the look and took the remote, putting it on the nightstand. "No one is watching."

Sophie breathed in. Okay, she thought. Stay cool. This was unexpected. But not unwelcome. Sure she wanted to spend more time with him. Wasn't expecting a fucking. Wasn't going to say no. He pulled the top of his jeans open. Had a hard-on under there. He kicked his boots off to the side of the bed and dropped his jeans. Seemed to be going a little quick. She did want to enjoy this, after all.

Jeans down and off while she watched, Will sat on the bed next to her. Reached over and cupped her face with his palm. Kissing her gently. Slowly. He moved her head with his hand, carefully, and started to kiss her neck. Just as she liked it. Okay. Fuck slowly. She reached down to his cock. Grabbed it in a fist through his boxers. Small. Huh. It was the same size as her ex. Somewhere in the back of her mind she imagined that Will would be hung like a stallion.

He shifted slightly, and she got a better grip.

Actually, wait. It was getting bigger. Wasn't properly hard yet. Rounder. Fatter. Okay. This felt far more impressive. Almost ... massive. Oi, oi. His lips left her neck and he moved, straddling her as she sat with her head to the pillows, the headboard. He was on his knees for a second. She saw it through his shorts. Looked like he might be hitting twelve inches. Fucking hell. She had only dreamt of a cock that size. And the dildo she had at home was about that.

She still had her hand on it. Realised it was at the base. So much more above her hand. She stroked up the huge length of it. Will pulled back, leaving her grip and shuffling down the bed. He took each of her ankles in his hand and pulled her down the bed until she was flat, head now on the pillow, Will towering over her. She gasped in anticipation as he pulled his t-shirt off over his head. His body *was sculpted*. Not massive bulk like a wrestler, but toned. Like Ryan Reynolds. Actually, in person, she could see some of Reynolds in Will. Just as he moved and turned. Never noticed it on camera before. Whatever. She reached over to take his cock in her hand again and he knocked her reach away. Let out a little snort. "Not yet," he whispered. He reached down under her long t-shirt and she felt him grip her panties. She was wearing good ones. Ever the optimist. He pulled them from her. Below the knees, and off. Then he was down, sliding his head under the top of the shirt. She could feel his breath on her skin, and then the touch of his tongue. It was like every fucking fantasy she'd ever had about the guy. Coming all at once.

Talking of coming …

Sophie reached up behind her head. This guy knew where to touch her. It was like magic. Like he was in her head, moving from where he was to where she wanted him without her actually having to say anything. Fucking hell. It was getting harder for her to concentrate as the ripple of pleasure radiated from where his tongue was out, warming her whole body until she started to shake. Boiling orgasm running over her. Will moved away just as it was becoming too much, but knew she wasn't finished. He got back to his knees. Pushed his shorts off. He rolled her helpless body over, and gripped her hips, lifting her up. He guided his cock into her with bizarre accuracy as he started to fuck her from behind.

It was like a fever dream.

He stretched her, his cock too big, but as the

motion started it felt better, like he fit just perfectly. Jesus fucking Christ, she was going to cum again. Like his cock was made of fucking magic. Had fingers on the end of it shmooshing her g-spot, or something. She clenched up as she came again, within seconds.

"Fucking damn it," she screamed at the top of her voice. Oh, well. The gig was up. Everyone in the house now knew she was fucking someone. She started groaning as she came again. Third times a charm. She pulled forward, sliding off his cock, unable to take it in there anymore. Face against the headboard. Heaving air in and out of her lungs. She was cold. Sweat on her face. Without turning around she knelt, her legs weak, struggling to keep her up. Best give something back. She pulled her t-shirt up over her head. Reached around behind her and unhooked her bra. Let it drop to the bed. She pushed her hand out behind her, felt his skin there. Naked, she turned, faced him, dropping her head down in one easy motion, ready to suck his cock.

Screamed as she saw a thousand tiny hands reaching towards her, coming from the shaft of Will's penis. They were all grabbing, fingers rolling to fists and back out like baby hands wanting sweets.

She looked up, her face contorted in horror, into the face of the Great Child. A baby, a six foot tall baby, snot dribbling out of its left nostril. Big chubby belly. Massive cock covered in hands. It reached forward. Baby arm. The length of an adults. "Mumma," it said, deep voiced like an adult.

Sophie couldn't take it. Vomit careened up her throat and dribbled out of her mouth. Not quite throwing up, so much as letting it drool out. The baby touched her face. Put its fingers into the sick, a burning smell, stomach acids coming from it. It reached up and sucked her vomit from its fat digits. Made a chirpy laughing sound. Sophie was crying. She screamed. Rolled from the bed, falling hard to her knees. The clunk of the floorboards as she landed. Grunting in pain. She turned onto her arse, pushing herself across the floor of the bedroom, tears streaking her face. Sick on her chest, her tits. She scooted backwards, towards the door. Back up against it. The Great Child was still on the bed, on it's knees. Cock hard. Reaching towards her, but unable to walk. It was glaring around, trying to find a way to get from the bed to her.

It was going to work out how to crawl eventually.

Sophie turned, her hand on the door handle already, twisting, trying to pull the door open as she leant against it. She rolled to the side. Screaming. Crying. Pulled open the door. Still on the floor. Crawling out into the hallway. She got up to her feet. Naked. Wiping the tears from her face with the back of her arm, snot, mixed with spit, tears. Vomit. Acidic, and burning. She crashed against the wall on the other side of the hall, unsteady on her feet for so many reasons. Moist legs from where she'd ejaculated. Shuddering. No control over her body. Screaming. Doors opening.

Larry was there first. He had his arms out, putting them around her. She fought him back. Forcing him off her. "What's going on?" he asked. Then there was Maria, Tracy. David stayed back. Kept his distance.

Sophie tried to pull air in. Stop hyperventilating. She pointed to her bedroom door. Let Maria wrap her arms around her. Larry looked worried, he glanced to David, hoping to get some backup from the boy, but still David held his ground.

Larry went to the door. Slowly. Terrified. You could see it in his eyes. Sophie buried her face in Maria's shoulder. Waiting for the scream to come.

It never did.

She pulled her face up. Off the nightshirt Maria was wearing, leaving behind a snail trail of bodily fluids, looking over to Larry. He was standing in the doorway. He'd been in the room. The lights were already on. He crossed to the en-suite. Checked in there.

There was nothing in the room.

No one. No Great Child.

No Will.

"You were just dreaming," Maria cooed, slowly. "A nightmare."

But Sophie could see her eyes as they drifted down her body to the wetness between her legs. She could see her judging her. *A dream.*

CHAPTER 8

So, they obviously thought she was mad. *Obviously*. Sophie pushed away from Maria. She hobbled into the bedroom doorway, weak. Ignored the slick on her legs. She pushed by Larry. Pretended that her nakedness wasn't there. Hopefully if she did, they would. She put her hand on his chest, as he stood in the doorway looking in, as she made it into the room. She gently pushed him backwards out into the hallway, observant for the first time that he was wearing button up pyjamas. He was also getting a good look at her. Fucker. She still had tears on her face. She was still slovenly from the fucking. They were all looking at her.

She turned into the room. Didn't close the door. She stormed across to the bathroom. Checked in. Nothing. What. The. Fuck. She glanced over to Larry, stood in the hallway now. Staring. Had his mouth open like he wanted to say something, but daren't, in case she realised he was staring and put some clothes on.

Dirty cunt.

"Well?" she blurted.

That seemed to snap Larry out of it and he suddenly looked at the floor. Turned away. Sophie walked over and slammed the door. She'd stopped crying now. Her face streaked with red. Fucking wet dream. Weird arse, fucking—literally—wet dream.

She looked up at the camera. Red light flashing. It was them. "What did you do?" she screamed into the lens. "What did you drug me with?" She hurried over to the bathroom and in. Turned the shower on. She put her hand under it to check the temperature, and then discarded the idea. Didn't care. She stepped in. Started washing. Washing the shame from her face. From in between her legs. She felt herself. With her fingers. She could feel that someone had been inside her. Still. Serious fucking hallucinogens. She washed her cum from her legs. Wetted her hair. Tried to feel right. The whole fucking group had gotten a look at her. Jesus. She should leave. Leave now, rather than face them all again.

Sophie stepped out the shower and dried quickly. Rudimentarily. If she left now, cancelled her Patreon, and never went into the forum again then nobody would be any the wiser. She'd just ghost the whole lot of them. But if she did that, she couldn't sue. For whatever they'd clearly drugged her with.

Why her?

Fucking fuck.

She left the bathroom. Didn't care that she was naked. She pulled her bra back on, then her knickers. T-shirt. Jeans. Shoes.

There was a knock at the door.

Made her jump a little. Then tense. "Are you okay?" It was Maria. "None of us can sleep now. We're going to go downstairs. You can come and talk. If you want." She added the *if you want* to the end with some reluctance, by the sound of it.

Shit. Sophie stood there for a second. That blew her idea of doing a bunk in the middle of the night. "Okay," she called back. Seemed non-committal enough, she supposed. She dropped down onto the bed. She looked at the sheets. Damp. Damp from her. No one else. Fucking hell. Drugged or not, she'd made a good fucking fool of herself.

Right, she thought. *Face them*. That way, no one can say you ran way.

Sophie got up. She watched as several shadows crossed the light in the crack at the bottom of the door. She waited a minute until she was sure they'd all left and gone downstairs, and then she followed.

CHAPTER 9

Sophie stood at the top of the stairs. She still didn't feel right. How she'd finger fucked herself like that in her sleep ... well. And it was all on camera. She looked up at the two camera's covering the stairs. Red lights flashing. *Motherfuckers*, she mouthed at them. She went down. Slowly. She'd left her bag in the room. *Stay for a while*, she'd said to herself. It was the only way to save face. Tell the truth.

And then I turned around and Will had turned into a giant baby with a horse sized cock that was covered in tiny child hands all reaching for me.

She wavered a little. Maybe she should leave out some of the details. Down the stairs. The door to the living room was open. So was the door to the kitchen. Could have been the beer. Or the sandwiches. Everyone had eaten something different. Drank something different. That must have been how they got her. She went down to the hallway and stuck her head in the kitchen. No one in there. Fine. She went to the fridge. Opened the door. Empty. What the fuck. This thing was crammed with food a couple of hours ago. She slammed the door. There had to be someone in there fucking with her. One of the others? Perhaps. Or someone else. It's not like they'd checked around the house, was it? Or maybe they had. After she'd fallen asleep in the living room. In front of the fire. Maybe they were all in on it, and this *ride* was just for her.

Sophie took in a deep breath. She could still taste puke. She turned the tap on the sink. Get a drink from that. No such luck. The water was out. *Fucking …* she started shaking. She was so angry. She turned and went out into the hallway. Across. To the living room. She pushed the door fully open and started. "Look," she said. "I know you all saw what you saw—" Stopped. No people. Nothing, in fact. Sophie. Looked around the room like they might have been hiding in the shadows. Where the fuck were they? Her eyes rested on the fire. It was out now. Must have burnt itself out. She went and sat on the edge of the chair she'd slept in earlier. She could smell something. Musty. Something like the room hadn't been used in years. How odd. She leaned forward and held her hand out towards the fireplace. There was no heat coming from it. Even odder. It was full force fire a few hours ago. Not even that. She sat back in her chair.

They must have come in there, because the newspaper from the hallway was on the table between the two chairs now. She glanced at it. *Four Dead.* Maybe she should keep it for prosperity. She listened. Tried to hear where the others were. They were fucking well down there somewhere. Must be in one of the other rooms. The library opposite the living room, or the other room. The one she hadn't been in. She looked up at the camera. "This is so fucked up," she said. "You better not be selling my naked body on the internet."

She didn't even know if they could hear her.

"Fuckers," she muttered under her breath, getting

up. She went back to the hallway. Still couldn't hear anything. Over to the door into the library. She pushed it open and went in. Checked for a camera in the darkness. Red light. All present and correct. But no people. Must be in the other room. She flicked the light on.

Well. She could wait for a moment. She let the door go. Swung closed. Sophie looked around the walls of books. There was a ladder on wheels like she'd seen in the films. And a spiral stair case made of wrought iron going up to a second floor, where a single walkway went around the outside of the room, allowing access to the rest of the books. Where there wasn't books, there was red. Lots of red. The floor was carpeted. It was different from the rest of the house. Somehow more welcoming. In there, too, was an open fire. Out. This one looked like it had never been lit. Unlike the other. Weird. Facing it, away from the rest of the room was a chair.

Probably for the old master to do his reading in. Had a small table next to it. She walked over to it. The chair was worn. It looked like it had been worn from years of love. The table had a blurry ring on it, where a glass of the finest brandy had been placed, each and every night, while he read. The glass, cooled by the ice, producing a single drop of condensation on the outside, running down.

She shook herself out of it.

Quite. She continued to wander the outside of the room taking in all the books. They looked fine. Expensive. They looked like they had been cared for and loved. She let her fingers dance along them, eventually reaching the spiral stairs to the landing of the upper of the room. She climbed them slowly. There was something regal—romantic even—about the place.

The thoughts of the drug induced baby rape slipping from her mind. Like it was all a dream.

She reached the top. Like a balcony, there was a handrail easily tall enough to stop her from feeling like she might fall, and just a walkway around the room, lined on one side with more books. Rows and rows of them. She looked down the spines at the titles. Dickens. Shakespeare. Dante. In the upper part of the room the smell was predominantly of bound leather. Sophie clutched at her bare arms and shivered. The cold, coming from nowhere.

She heard something below. Looked over the edge of the handrail to the door. It was still closed. And then the light of the fire caught her eye. She looked to the other side of the room. The fire, burning hard, like it had been started by a professional, stoked to within an inch of its life. She couldn't see who, but there was someone sitting in the chair. She could see the feet of a man. Trousers. Shoes. "Larry?" she called out quietly.

There was no reply, and the man didn't move.

"David?" This time the words escaped her even more quietly.

A hand came from the man, from behind the shallow wings of the chair, holding a glass over the table. Dark brown spirit. On the rocks. Sophie drew in a breath. It was like she *knew*. She gripped the rail as she felt herself become weak, and waited for the lightness in her head to pass. The glass clonked as it touched the hard, polished wood. Sophie crept back along to the spiral set of stairs and started down. She cursed herself as her shoes made light tapping noises on the ironwork of the steps.

As she reached the bottom, she looked between the back of the chair and the door. Halfway between the two. Part of her wanted to see who was in the chair. Part of her wanted to flee. They hadn't drugged her this time. She *knew* they hadn't. She hadn't had anything that could have been spiked. She could scream. Bring the others. But she wasn't sure where they were. She hadn't heard them. What made her think that they might hear her?

No.

It was better to leave.

She turned towards the door, bracing herself before hurrying, when the man in the chair stood.

CHAPTER 10

The man stood, turning as he did. He was tall. Almost monstrously so. He was wearing a suit, tattered. She could only see his flesh on his face and hands, but both were smeared with blood, dull, like it had been there a long time. A bald head, dark eyes.

She paid little attention, almost stumbled, as she ran towards the door, letting out a dull scream, caught in her throat.

The man raised his hand. Sophie heard the latch of the lock turn inside the wood of the door, locking her in the room with him. She staggered to a stop and turned, slowly. He still had his arm up. He turned it to her and she lifted. From the carpet. Just enough that the toes of the shoes still touched the fabric beneath. She tried to scream out, but there was nothing there. His hold, it seemed to encapsulate her. Lifting her up, but she couldn't feel the pressure anywhere.

Like the wind was carrying her.

Then he moved his hand, gesturing her forward, her toes dragging on the carpet as she floated to him.

As she got closer, she saw what had caused the blood on him. He was tied in wire, draped around him, circling his skin, pulled tight until it had cut into him, dug into his flesh. The Bound Man had trenches in his skin, blood slipping from them, blood, over blood. Dark sticky, dried, blood beneath slick fresh blood. Wrapped, was every inch of skin she could see. And she assumed it continued beneath the dark grey suit he wore.

Sophie struggled to get free of his grip. Whatever fucking magic this was that held her up. Her mind racing, trying to focus on the fact—*it was a fact*—that she must have been drugged again. This shit wasn't real. Wasn't possible.

She looked into his face. The wire, wrapped around and around him, distorting his true features made him look like a monster. Taut into his skin on his face, digging down to his skull, his jaw. He smiled beneath the painted bloody skin, his mouth barely able to be opened.

But it could.

Sophie tried to move her hands. She could roll her fingers, but couldn't get her arms from beside her body. She couldn't raise them to strike out at him.

He lifted his head. The wires cut into his throat, tight, the flesh bulging on each side of it, and the blood running faster, harder, down, inside his suit, his shirt, white, staining with each movement, bloody, sticking to his body. He whispered, "The time," in a hush.

Sophie screamed. This time it released from her body, coming like a boom.

And The Bound Man laughed.

He pulled his tie loose. Taking it over his head. Unbuttoning his shirt until it hung loose. His whole body a drench. His skin yawning and tearing with his movements, bleeding more. Harshly. Viscous, slick.

The smell of metal filled the room. As did the sound of his wheezing as he struggled to move, almost as imprisoned as she was.

He pushed the shirt from his shoulders, and undid the cuffs.

Sophie struggled—thrashed—, tiring, as she fought to gain some control over her body, but she was still held there, above the carpet. She watched as he undressed so fucking casually, undressing for bed, changing for the opera. Gore splattered. Vile. Tears streamed down her face. She was whispering, whimpering. "Please God, no. Enough. I don't want to be here anymore."

The Bound Man undid his belt, slipped it from the rings in his trousers. Taking it, folded.

He walked around behind her. She tried to turn. To follow. She could tell from the way he held the leather that his intention was to beat her with it. There was no way he was holding it like that if he wasn't going to.

They were going too far.

"No," she screamed. She looked up to the camera. "Please, fucking hell. No." the words were barely audible from the crying, the tears on her face, drooling into her mouth. Spit dribbling from her maw.

"Time," came the whisper again. Hoarse. Rough. The wires digging into the monsters vocal cords.

"Please," she said quietly.

The Bound Man pushed himself up against her

back. He was tall enough that even with her suspended in the air, his head was at the same height as hers. She could smell him. Not only his blood, iron and mercury, but his decomposing flesh beneath. Like he'd been trapped, bleeding for an eternity. He reached around from behind, his sloppy, wet, hand running over her clothes. Leaving behind the stains of his touch. His breathing quickened as he enjoyed her shape beneath his bloody skin.

She watched him probe his fingertips around her stomach, trailing down to the button on her jeans. Then up, to her breasts. She held her breath. His flesh so close to hers. The smell. The blood. His wheezing enjoyment. She cried out. His hand slid under her t-shirt. Onto her bare flesh. She could feel his wet fingers as they rode up her body to her bra. Teasing the edges. Leaving moist imprints.

She struggled to no avail.

The Bound Man suddenly pushed his fingers under her bra. Onto the warm flesh of her breast. Pinching her nipple. She kicked. Tried to. Couldn't move. She could hear him breathe harder. Almost touch the enjoyment he was feeling. He withdrew. Slid his hand back down her belly. To the button on her jeans. He popped it open. Blood oozing down beneath.

Sophie stopped crying. Suddenly it all seemed to suck back up inside her. She found herself breathing in more than out. Sucking the air in. Holding it. Her face wet, she closed her eyes as he unzipped her jeans and pulled them down. All with that one bloody hand.

She stopped trying to fight it.

It was no fucking use anyway.

She felt the denim pulled from her skin. Her shoes off, too.

She could feel the warmth of the fire on her legs. He touched the front of her knickers. Gently. His push plagued the short hair she had beneath. She had air in her lungs now. She held it there. Too afraid to let it out.

He laughed.

A short sickening little laugh. Choked out as he struggled to speak, the destruction of his body, enduring.

He stepped backwards. Away from her. She couldn't smell him anymore.

A snap.

A slap.

Sophie felt a numbness across the back of her legs, on the firm part below her arse. Then quickly, a warmth came. A burning. A heat. A *searing*. The air escaped her, she had no choice. Screamed out. "Fucking hell." The pain of a thousand burns rattled through her body as he whipped her again with the belt against her bare skin. The leather cutting into her, taking the first layer of her skin. Wetness, weeping from her. On the backs of her calves. Drawing down towards her feet.

The tears came again.

"Please," she muttered. "What do you want?"

"Flesh," came the rasping reply. "It has been so long."

Then he whipped her again. The pain returned, from numbness came fire. Riding up her legs into her stomach. Vomit rolling around in her gut, again. "No," she begged, fighting to stay conscious as the fear, pain, hate, fought against her. "It must be a nightmare," she said. The Bound Man made some hissed laugh, quietly.

Then the fire again.

Sophie drooped, losing the will to continue to fight. She just let herself be held there. And that seemed to be enough to stop him. He returned to her, to her back, and brought his lukewarm body heat to hers. He ran his fingers down the backs of her legs. She could feel the uneven flesh there, as he rode over welts and cuts, skin pulled up, torn away.

"So warm," he said. His hand moving up again. Cupping her between her legs. Then around. Up. Onto her torso. He tossed the belt away. Over to the chair, onto it. Came around in front of her. He pulled a knife. She wasn't composed enough to see where it had come from.

Then he cut her t-shirt from her.

She hung. Only in her underwear. As he watched. In silence.

She could hear the dripping of her blood from the backs of her feet. Pooling on the carpet below. He could too. Watched her legs and feet.

He was hard, beneath his trousers. She could see.

Her head hung low, flopping down onto her chest. Not having the strength to hold it up. She tried to beg. Plead. But nothing came out. She was beaten. Worn down. He pulled open his trousers. Naked beneath. Blood drenched on the inside. Oozing through to the outside, through the material. Staining the charcoal grey to black. She shook her head. It was all she had.

He stepped forward naked. The wires covered him. Wrapping his torso, legs. Every part of him bled, fresh, an unending amount of blood, trailing out of him. More blood than could ever have been contained in a single meat-suit. Blood on the carpet. His. Hers. On him. Running freely from him. His cock. Hard. Wrapped as tight as the rest of him. Warm slick, red. Blood coming from his urethra. Like he was pissing it. She glanced up to his face, not wanting to see, but *having* to.

Grinning. Like a hyena. A jackal. Blood stained teeth.

Fuck.

He stepped over to her. Had the knife. He slid it under the edge of her knickers. Pulled it back away from her thigh. Cut them off. They dropped away. Sophie pushed her legs together. Hard as she could. Made the muscles burn. Tears on her face. No scream in her mouth this time.

Fear had taken it.

"No," she muttered.

The Bound Man moved the knife up to her bra. Cut that off too. She was naked. Hanging there in front of him, unable to move. He was still hard. Seemed to be getting off on the fact she was still fighting in whatever way she could. To stop him from touching her. Raping her.

"Police," she whispered. "You can't do this."

He stepped back, admired her, and then came forward. He had the knife out forwards, and dug the point of it to where her legs met. Just below her hair. Needled it inwards. "If you fight, it will cut."

Sophie didn't care. She kept her legs clamped shut. No way was she parting them for him.

The Bound Man twisted the knife. She felt the blade cut into the soft flesh of her inner thigh. She instinctively parted her legs. Moved them away from the source. Then his hand was there. Touching her flesh. Still tender from before.

"No," she screamed. "Help me." He moved his fingers around, slipping around her flesh, but never quite entering her. He stepped back. Releasing her. He looked down. Could see the blood from his hand on her skin. Beyond that the blood on the floor that had come from her.

He turned away. Walked back over to the chair. He stared at the fire for a moment. "Warmth," he hissed. Then he turned back. Had the belt again.

"No." She shook her head. "No*nonono*."

He strode to her. Placed his hand on her hair. Below her belly. "Choose." He stepped back.

Grabbed his cock. Pulled the foreskin back on it. The wires cutting deep into the flesh, blood pumping out harder and faster as he touched himself.

"The belt," she cried.

The Bound Man let himself go, staying to attention. He walked around behind her. She braced herself.

Slap.

Sting.

Numb.

Burn.

This time it was on her back. Below the shoulder blades. In the fleshy part. She screamed out. Pain blistered through her. She wailed.

He hit her again.

Again.

The blood wept down her back. The warmth of it relieving her at first, then the stinging taking her. She felt him. Close. Smelt him. His aroma different. He didn't just smell of blood metals now. The heady stench of dirty cock was in there too. "I lied," he said. His hand pushed the flesh of her arse apart, and she felt his fingers probing her arsehole.

Sophie screamed again, fought to move.

He was touching her anus. The blood acting as a lube. In to her rectum. She could feel his fingers moving about, discovering. He withdrew. Breathing hard. Wheezing loudly.

"What do you want?" she asked.

"Warmth. Freedom."

Sophie fell forward, onto the carpet, onto her knees. The blood on the carpet had started to clot, splashing up, black and red chunks of discarded human fluid, some cold like bloody custard. She turned. Unconcerned with either the goo she was kneeling in, or the fact that she had scooted onto her arse to face him.

But he wasn't there.

She looked around the room. The library. She was alone. Naked. On the carpet. Blood everywhere. Pain. *Everywhere.*

CHAPTER 11

The door crashed open. Larry. Of course it was fucking Larry. Sophie screamed. She tried to push herself out of the cooling, pooling blood, slipping and sliding on the rug. Slick. Cold. Oily. She tried to cover herself at the same time.

Larry stood there with his mouth open. David up close behind him. He looked like he was trying to see around Larry. Ogling her body. Beaten. Raped. Bloody. She picked her cut t-shirt from the blood and held it up against herself. It was sticky. "Get out," she screamed. So confused.

Sophie looked around on the floor for her clothes. Her knickers, bra. T-shirt. They were all fucked. She picked up her jeans, dropping the t-shirt. Started to pull them on.

Maria was at the door. "Fuck off," she was saying to Larry and David. They might have been perving. They might have been in some shock. Impossible to tell. Sophie dragged the blood wet jeans up her legs as they clung to the skin. She was shaking. Crying.

Maria came over as Tracy pushed the others out of the room. "You heard her," she was barking at them.

Maria came straight to Sophie's side. Pulled her sweatshirt off without thought and handed it to her.

Sophie held it. Weeping. "I'll get blood on it," she said.

"Give a fuck," Maria answered. She helped Sophie with the shirt, over her head.

Tracy slammed the door and went over to her. "What happened?" she asked quietly. She was looking at the rug. The blood. The blood that was everywhere. "Who did this?"

"I don't know." Sophie was shaking all over. Barely able to speak. "He beat me."

"Was it Larry?" Tracy looked back to the door. "I will cut him—"

"No," Sophie blurted, interrupting. "It was someone ... something ... else. Barely human."

Maria picked up Sophie's knickers and held them up, cut with a blade. "Who?" she asked.

Sophie looked over to the chair. The knife. The belt. Gone. "I ..." she looked at the table. The glass was still there. She broke away from Maria and picked it up. It was still cold from the ice. Sniffed it. Whiskey. She showed the two of them. "Look. It was real. This was his."

Maria looked up at the camera. "Enough," she shouted into the corner of the room. "End this now." She shook her head, and took Sophie's arm. Dragging her across to the door.

Sophie could barely keep herself up on her legs. Her jeans chaffed against the wounds on her flesh.

"Come on." She threw the door open and pulled Sophie into the hallway.

Tracy followed. She stopped as Maria let Sophie

steady herself on the table. "Where did the boys go?"

Maria glanced around. "If they've got anything to do with this, I will have them in court." She spun around looking for the cameras. "And you," she screamed. "You can't do this." She went to the front door and grabbed the handle. Twisted it back and forth. "Fuckers have locked us in." She turned back into the hall. "Larry? Dave?" she shouted.

No reply.

"If they're in on this," she muttered.

Sophie faced the table. She had her hands palm flat on it, staring down. Everything in the room was passing her by. She wanted to go home. The paper was there. Again. *Three Dead*. She frowned.

"Here," Tracy said, crossing to the living room. She looked in. "This." She went into the room and returned a few seconds later with the small table from between the chairs. She brought it up like she was going to fight a tiger. "You open this door up, or we're breaking out." She waved the table at the camera. Red light flashed.

Nothing more.

She ran at the door, wielding the table like a club and slammed it against the glass in the top half of it. The table clunked. The crack of wood. The table lost its solidity, fracturing under the strength of the glass. She let it drop to the ground. "What the fuck?" Tracy raised her boot. DMs. She kicked the door. The glass even. Nothing. Not so much as a crack.

Maria stopped her. Put her arm out and calmed

her. "Leave it," she said. "There must be a back door." She went to Sophie, put her arm around her. "You okay to move?"

Sophie nodded. She felt like she had the mother of all hangovers.

"Wasn't one in the kitchen," Tracy said. "What about this one?" She went over to the last door in the hallway that they had yet to try. The door next to the living room. She opened it. Beyond was a set of stairs. Leading down to the basement.

"Fuck that," Sophie said. "I'm not going down into the dark." She pushed away from Maria. "Not with those things in here."

CHAPTER 12

Tracy pulled her phone out. "Fuck this." She started thumbing the screen. "We're out of here."

Before she'd gotten anywhere close to dialling, it started to ring.

Everyone's phone started to ring.

Tracy answer it. "Will," she barked down at the screen. "Get us the fuck outta here. We've had it."

He laughed down the phone at her. "I'm sorry, all."

By now Maria had answered hers, but Sophie's phone was still ringing. She couldn't be bothered to join the group chat, instead just letting it bellow to itself. She slowly, sorely, rounded Maria and looked down at Will's face on her screen. She looked at the chat attendees. The boys hadn't joined. "What the fuck?" Sophie shouted.

"Wow," he replied. He was grinning like a buffoon. "You really are a screamer."

"Cunt," she muttered.

Will raised his eyebrows. "Language." She could hear the chuckle below his voice. "Anyhow. You'll find that your phones won't dial out. Jammers and blockers and such. Don't ask me the deets on that one. My I.T. guy deals with all that."

"What's going on?" Maria asked. Her voice

shook as she spoke.

Will made this quiet tutting sound. "I'm surprised you haven't cobbled together some theory. Bunch of women locked up together." He laughed.

"Twat," Maria expounded.

"It's quite simple really. You've seen the state of the place. It's due for demo. Obviously. People keep going missing here, so they decided to knock the place down. That's why there's no furniture. Although I can't believe that you've all been sleeping on the floor."

Maria shot a look to Tracy and then to Sophie, frowning. Sophie stared back at her. Well. Fucking hell.

"Anyway," Will continued. "Greased a few palms, and you can get a couple of uninterrupted days with a haunted house. See, *they* thought some whack job serial killer was lurking about the place. We didn't. We never thought such a thing. Fucking obvious when you do your research. Well, we *thought* it wasn't a serial killer. Wouldn't really have mattered if it was, to be honest. Am I right?"

Sophie shook her head. "But why?" she asked quietly.

"Ah, Soph. Lovely Soph."

She hated being call fucking *Soph*.

"Should have jumped a few more levels, shouldn't you? The one hundred pound Patreon level is our perfect hunting ground. All those conversations? You clearly wanted the um, d. Is that right?"

Fucking douche.

"Made you easy to profile. Most people have to be in the one hundreders for a few months at least until we work out if they're easily ... disposable. But you couldn't wait to tell me the ins and outs of your messy break up, could you? Wanting a bit of the ol' Will. Heh. So you sort of jumped to the front of the queue."

"You are never getting this," Sophie said, cold, but quiet.

"I never wanted it, whore." Will grinned into the phone.

"What was the point?" she asked.

"You see, if you'd jumped up to the five hunderders you'd have missed out on the fun all together. The cameras—they're recording for a private show. *The Private Show*. You will have seen it on the Patreon board. The fivers get a private show every six or nine months. Something that they only see, no one before them and no one after. You're Junes'."

"You're fucking us up for a private show?"

"Yeah. Usually we have to manufacture this sort of shit, but you lot seem to be doing perfectly well on your own. So the doors are locked. There's no way out. And the whole group is going to see you wandering about naked, love." He killed the call.

Tracy looked over to the two of them. "What a cunt."

Sophie nodded. "But he's not doing it. He just *thinks* he is."

"Huh?" Maria grunted.

"He said there was no furniture, right?" She tapped on the table in the middle of the room. The paper was gone. Again. "I didn't get fucked by a giant baby on the floor."

Maria screwed her face up.

"You heard."

"Are you okay?"

Sophie looked down at herself. Blood streaked her skin. Her back and legs stung as the loose flesh became tacky, sticking to the clothes she wore. Blood clotting in the folds of Maria's sweatshirt. "Do I look okay?" she asked.

Tracy bobbed her head from side to side. "Got a point. So what *is* going on?"

"Fucking place is haunted. Clearly." Sophie glanced between the two of them, then to the stairs. "We find the boys and we find a way out. There's no way Cunty and Cuntier fixed this door so that a table would bounce off it, so I say whatever is haunting this place is in control. So we work on that, and deal with the podcasters later."

"I must say," Maria said, looking Sophie up and down, "you're taking this awfully well."

It was Sophie's turn to head bob. "I'm just staying focussed on cutting Will's tiny prick off and feeding it to him."

"Reasonable." Tracy turned to the stairs. "Shall we?"

CHAPTER 13

At the top of the stairs, the three of them waited. Sophie was trying to justify in her mind which door to open first. They were all closed. The others seemed to be behind her, waiting for her to do something. *Again*.

But there was no time for petty arguments about who was in charge.

"Which rooms were yours?"

"Ours were the two at the end," Maria said.

Sophie's was the one closest to the stairwell. That meant the boy's rooms were probably in the middle. The most likely place for them to be now. *Most likely*.

"Why don't we call out?" Maria said.

"You fucking stupid?" hissed Tracy. "Don't want to advertise our presence."

Maria looked at her with a face that said, *the fuck?* But she didn't speak.

Sophie ignored them and went down to the middle door, on the left. She wished she had a weapon, but wasn't sure what in the house was real and what wasn't any longer. She just knew the pain was real. She rapped quietly on the door as the other two joined her. "Whose door is this?" she whispered.

The two of them looked at each other. Maria made a noise like dishwater emptying, before saying, "David?" She didn't sound at all sure.

Sophie raised her hand to knock again, but stopped. She changed her mind. Grabbed the handle and opened it.

The door swung open. The lights inside, off. The darkness broken by the lights from the hallway. Instinctively Sophie looked up to the corner. Red light. She stepped forward, just letting her feet touch the shadow. Her hand up to the side. Fumbled for a light switch and flicked it on.

Maria was the closest behind her. She breathed in, slow. Deep. As if her lungs never ended.

David was suspended over the bed. Held in some sort of sex swing. He was hung facing downwards, his face staring down towards the pillows of the bed, but not touching it. He was gagged. Ball gag. His eyes open. But not moving. He hung limp, his legs belted apart, his arse in the air. His hands out to the side. Some macabre doll, hung like a marionette for the pleasure of—Sophie guessed—The Bound Man. The Great Child was a rapist cunt, but didn't seem overly … flexible.

There was a *hurk* sound, and Maria tipped forward throwing up the contents of her stomach. Bile and fish stinking shit slopped onto the floor. *Fuck*. Sophie sidestepped so that it didn't run over her feet. She noticed, looking down, that she had blood on her shoes that had come from up her jeans. The pain was getting worse. It was like the act itself had numbed her, and the feeling was now returning. She was going to need painkillers. Lots of them.

Sophie stepped across the room towards the

corpse. She could see better from there. David was naked in the swing. His arse had something sticking from it. The blade. The Bound Man. She wanted to take it out. Give the poor boy some dignity back. But she didn't want to touch it, either. The sheets below him were drenched in his blood. Gooey, wet. The man was a master at spilling that, for sure. Sophie looked at David's skin. Pale. His gloop on the outside, rather than where it should have been.

She turned back to the door.

Tracy was holding Maria's hair back as she spat the last of her vomit onto the floor.

She went back to the door and flicked the light out. "Better see if Larry fared any better," she said with a sigh.

The three of them back out in the corridor, Sophie pulled the door closed behind her. "Either of you have any painkillers?" Tracy opened her bag and pulled out a small plastic bag. There were some pills in it. Sophie looked from the baggie to Tracy. Raised her eyebrows.

"What?" Tracy said. "They're just co-codomol. I didn't have anything else to bring them in." She dragged a massive frown. "Stereo-typing much."

Sophie shook her head. "Sorry. Thank you." She took the bag and tipped two out. Then another two. Took all four dry. Absolutely fucking filthy taste, especially when she had to crunch them. Blerg. She nodded again to Tracy. Apology. Then went over to Larry's door.

Didn't bother knocking this time.

She pushed the door open without warning.

The light was on in Larry's room. He was hanging in the air, next to the bed. Suspended in the nothing, much as Sophie was in the library. The Bound Man was behind him. The Great Child was sitting on the floor in the corner of the room. The child was watching. It was sat naked, it's giant baby legs crossed in front of it. It was reaching forward towards Larry, like it wanted to grab him. Hug him.

The Bound Man was fucking Larry.

At least that was what it looked like.

As soon as the door was fully open it knocked against the wall, and The Bound Man's attention was grabbed. He looked to the noise. Then to the three women standing there. Then he was gone. Disappeared like a spirit. Larry dropped to the floor like a discarded toy.

The Great Child screamed. Noise like a baby having had it's dummy taken away, but amplified to the volume of a dire wolf wanting dinner.

Sophie hurried into the room towards Larry. Got no more than half way from the door to the bed, when The Great Child disappeared like the man.

"What the fuck ..." Tracy whispered. Maria turned back, stumbling across the hallway to the wall opposite, and doubled over like she was going to puke again, but nothing came forward.

Sophie went to Larry's side. He wasn't moving.

Crouched. Touched him. She rolled him over onto his back. There was no physical signs of torture or torment. But he was clearly dead. His eyes were open. He stared into space. Sophie dragged the sheet from the bed and covered him. Went back to the door.

Tracy watched her without moving. "Now what?"

Sophie took a deep breath. "The boys are dead and there's no way out. Has every room up here been looked through?"

Tracy looked to Maria, pale, leaning against the wall. She made a semi-coherent denial. Possibly.

CHAPTER 14

Sophie pulled the door to Larry's room closed and the three of them stood in the hallway. Sophie counted out the doors. "What about that one?" There was one door that hadn't been accounted for.

"We went in there earlier. It was empty."

"Totally. Not even any carpet," Maria agreed.

Sophie put her finger up in the air. "Doesn't mean anything now, does it?" She strode over to the door. The pain in her back and legs had eased. The overabundance of strong painkillers seemed to have done the trick. But she knew it was a mess back there. She could feel Maria's sweatshirt sticking and peeling off as she moved. The tightness of her jeans clamped on the splits in the skin. Probably fused on by now. She was going to need to go to the hospital before going home. If she got out of this. She opened it, pushing the door inwards.

A brightly lit office. A study of sorts. Warm. Warmer than the rest of the house. Sophie shook her head.

Maria came up to her side, looking in. "How did you know?"

"Didn't." She stepped in. "Just lucky, I guess." The room was carpeted. Now. There was a writing desk in the middle of the far wall, facing the wall. Antique looking thing. There was a bookshelf on the side. Had some books on it, but nothing like those in the library. They looked expensive. These looked tatty. She walked across to the desk. Pulled the chair out. Ratty. Looked like the moths had been at it. It was old. Hard wood. Brown. Same as the desk. There was paperwork scattered across it. She went to sit, to read, to take some of the weight off her legs. Felt like she'd run a fucking marathon. Then she thought better of it. Probably would hurt like shit. She flicked through the papers.

"What is it?" Tracy asked. She was standing at the bookshelf looking at the books.

"Ownership papers for the house." She glanced down the documents. Some were typed. Most were hand written. "Henry Hodder."

Tracy pulled a book out and opened it. She guided her eyes with her index finger down a page. "This is a book on genealogy. Real old one, too." She placed it back on the shelf.

"Weird," Sophie said. She held the papers. Looked around the room. The heat was coming from a duct. Must be a furnace in the basement. She stared at it for a moment. "This room is weird."

"No shit," said Maria from the doorway. She was looking out. Keeping some sort of guard. Against what—or what she thought she was going to do about it if anything turned up—Sophie didn't know.

"No. All the other rooms were heated by radiators, right?" She looked over to Tracy for agreement. She shrugged—no idea. "No," Sophie continued. "They were. All the other rooms we've seen have been modern. The kitchen. The fridge. The library and the living room. They were done out old looking, but stank of expensive period furniture. Reproduction shit." She glanced to Maria, who was also just staring at her. "This room feels like we've stepped back in time, doesn't it?"

Tracy looked around. She looked at the carpet. The curtains pulled closed at the window. The wallpaper. She tilted her head to the side. "I guess."

Sophie looked back at the papers in her hand. "Why? Why does it feel like we're inside Hodder's house in the past?" She licked her finger and started flipping through the papers. Ownership documents. And birth, marriage and death documents. Registration papers. She looked at the names. "Hodder had a wife. A kid."

Tracy joined her at the desk. "When?"

"Eighteen fifty. According to the death certificate the baby died at four months."

"Shit." Tracy took the paper and scanned down it. "Cause of death … infection."

"It's a reasonable reason." Sophie said.

"Then why are you frowning?" Tracy was staring at her.

"Why are we not leaving?" Asked Maria from the door. "How is this helping?" She pulled her phone from her pocket again and jabbed at the screen. Held it to her head. Shook her head. Pushed the phone back in her pocket. She looked at the two of them, dejected. "Nothing." Shrug.

"Come on." Sophie hurried across the room and out into the corridor. "Your room?" she asked Maria.

She pointed to one of the other doors.

Sophie opened it. The room was empty apart from Maria's bag. The backpack she was wearing when they'd arrived. The bed. Furniture. Gone. Maria drew a deep breath in. "Well, fucking hell." She stepped in and grabbed the bag, slinging it over her shoulder.

"Quite." Sophie turned back down the hallway to the stairs. "Come on." She hurried off.

CHAPTER 15

The three of them returned to the ground floor of the house. Maria dumped her bag at the bottom of the stairs. Sophie went to the living room. Opened the door. "Empty," she said, closing it again. Over to the library. Pushed the door open. "Ah," she said.

She went in, followed by the other two.

"What is it …?" Tracy's voice drifted off as she went into the room and looked around. The library was no more. There was different *everything*. The radiators on the walls, gone, replaced with the ducting and heating of a furnace. The dark, melancholy décor had been replaced with bright colours. The fireplace was empty, clean. The reading chair gone. Replaced with a cot. In it, a baby, stirring.

Tracy went to move forward towards the child, but Sophie stopped her. "Wait," she said.

She looked at her. "What the fuck is going on?" she asked. "Why's the room changed?"

"It's Hodder," Sophie replied. "He's tired. From the boys," she whispered. "Someone else has control of the house." She looked to the cot. Around the room. The ceilings high, but there was no spiral stairs up, now, just wallpapered. Old wallpaper.

A man walked out from behind them. There was nowhere he could have come from. He just appeared. He was a middle-aged man. Dressed in what looked like refinery from a hundred or more years ago. It was clear to Sophie he was The Bound Man. Before. The three of them drew back. Wary, before realising he couldn't see them. He wasn't The Bound Man, but an image from a time gone.

He walked to the cot. Gently picked up the baby. He held it out in front of him so that the two of them faced each other. He was moving his lips but no sound could be heard.

"What the fuck is going on?" asked Maria.

"Watch." Sophie stared onward, transfixed.

The man whispered his nothings to the child for a minute, maybe longer, before his face contorted into some sort of anger. He was shouting now, although they could still hear nothing.

Suddenly the fireplace crackled into life, untouched. It just *became*. Hodder walked over to it, holding the baby. He stood, by the open fire, and pulled the wrapped blanket from the child. There was a woman there now. She had run into the room. Pleading.

All in silence.

She had black hair. Tied back, tight. The resemblance to Sophie wasn't lost on her. The woman dropped to her knees, her arms out. She was beckoning for the man to pass her the child. He looked at her, angry, at first, then in some distain. His eyes moved to the child and his face morphed to a smile. A thin one. He looked at the fire. Bent forward.

Maria covered her eyes. "I can't," she said.

Sophie was pretty fucking sure he was going to toss the baby into the flames, too.

But he took a poker from the side of the fire. Held it like a club first, then waved it in the woman's face like a sword. Berating her.

Sophie wished she could hear what was being said.

Then he raised the poker, up, over his head. Brought it down on the woman. Struck her. Hard. She collapsed to the floor. Unmoving. The child was crying. Holding it's hand out towards the woman on the floor. Hodder raised the poker again. Brought it down on the woman. Again. Again.

Breaking the bone. Tearing the flesh.

Then she disappeared. Like she wasn't needed in the story anymore.

Hodder straightened. He tossed the poker, still slick with the woman's blood, into the fire, stabbing it in, so that the handle protruded. He looked down on the baby. Screaming. Crying. Tears on its face. All in silence. Hodder was talking. Pacifying the child. Waiting.

Waiting.

Sophie looked from the two of them to the cot. Then the fire. She was slowly shaking her head. "Don't watch," she whispered.

Hodder bounced the baby a few times as he cradled it, naked, in his arms. He was smiling now, properly, like he meant it. The child stopped crying, unaware—with no understanding—of what the monster had done to the woman. He walked the room. Circling.

Waiting.

Eventually returning to the fire. He took the child, holding it around its neck. Lifting it up, above the fireplace. The baby started crying and screaming again as Hodder held it out.

Sophie glanced across the room. The far corner. In it now sat The Great Child. It was leaning against the wall. Fat giant legs out in front of it. It was watching Hodder like a TV show. She looked back to the man. Holding the baby up. She could see from the corner of her eye that the other two had stopped watching. Turned away. But she couldn't. She stared on.

Hodder held the child out, as he bent, gripped the handle of the poker, sticking out of the flames. He pulled it, up. The end of it glowed, harsh, orange. Burning. He held it close to himself and the baby. The child was crying. Strangled under the man's grip.

He turned the baby to a horrific angle, holding it by the neck until it was facing away from him. Almost laying belly down along his arm.

Arse towards him.

Sophie looked down at Hodder. He was hard in his trousers. Fucker was getting off on it.

He drew back the poker and holding it like a rapier, touched the burning fire end of it on the baby's bare skin. The flesh moved and warped, smoke rising from it.

Then came a howling. The Great Child reached forward, unable to move across the room and sustain its own weight, the child screamed out watching Hodder torture the baby.

She looked back to the man. He lifted the poker from the baby's skin and it pulled up, stuck to it, slowly ripping it, peeling it from the child's body. The baby screamed silently, as its giant counterpart wailed so loud.

Sophie watched Hodder pull the poker back, and the shove the thing forward, into the child. Into the baby's tiny arsehole. She screamed at the suddenness of it, turning her head away to the side, only to be left looking at the giant baby. Wailing. Screaming. Reaching forward. "Fucking …" her words drifted off.

Maria tugged at the arm of Sophie's sweatshirt. "I want to go," she was saying. Crying.

Sophie looked back into the room.

Empty.

Nothing.

Even The Great Child was gone. The room was bare. Floorboards. Ripped, torn, and damaged wallpaper, untouched for years.

"Fucking cunt was a murderer."

"Who?" Tracy asked. She was still looking at the floor.

"Hodder. He killed his family."

"That's what you took from that?" she asked.

Sophie nodded. "And the newspapers. They kept changing. The child. I think the child has been trying to help us. The papers were all the reports of the missing people. People that Hodder has taken while they've been … here."

"Didn't the baby rape you?"

Sophie shot a glance to Maria. "Perhaps," she said, quiet. "It doesn't seem to have much control. Or power."

"What the fuck are you talking about?" Maria asked. Then she turned to Tracy. "What is she talking about?"

"No," Tracy said. "I get it. I think. The baby is controlling the old sections of the house. Cunt Will said the house was empty right? But we're seeing some modern shit, and some old time shit. The old time shit is the baby trying to warn us. Remembering only what it does from its life. Short life."

"And the visions that are controlling us. What we eat. Pain. Fucking. That's all Hodder. Playing with us."

Maria looked between the two of them. "So how do we get out?" She nodded along with her own words.

"The only place we haven't been is the basement."

"You really think that's a good idea?" she asked.

"Choice?" Sophie said, sombrely.

CHAPTER 16

"Fucking bollocks." Maria was staring down the stairs into the basement. "I don't see a light switch."

Sophie was leaning against the doorframe just to her side. "Look," she said. "I'm starting to feel a little queasy. I need out. Down is out. Has to be." She was sure it was the blood loss. Possibly overdosing on painkillers. Of which she wanted some more.

Tracy took the first step onto the stairs. She squinted down into the darkness. "I can feel a warm air coming up."

"The furnace?" Maria asked.

"Reasonable assumption, but isn't that fake baby ghost reality? Not *real* reality." Sophie said, quietly.

"Fucking bollocks," Maria said again.

"Come on." Tracy started down the stairs. Pulled out her phone and turned on the torch. The light cut weakly through the darkness. "This does not work like a film torch." Sophie did the same, followed by Maria.

Once the three of them had their lights on it didn't seem quite so bad. "See any cameras?" Sophie asked.

"There."

Sophie didn't know where Tracy had seen one, couldn't see her pointing, but she was fine knowing they were still on camera. "When we get out of here, I am so cutting Will up."

"I'll help," Tracy replied.

"Uh-huh." That was Maria.

Sophie found herself at the base of the stairs. Shining her light around she saw Maria still on them. Tracy was a few feet away to the other side of them. The basement was huge. It was impossible to tell how large, the expanse shrouded in blackness. She turned on the spot, the light out in front. There was a lingering feeling that something or someone was going to come up behind her. She would have felt better if she could have mapped out the basement. No idea of where it started, where it stopped.

"What's this?" Tracy. Over to the side.

Sophie turned. She flashed the light up on Maria still stood on the stairs at the bottom. Then followed across to Tracy. She was on the other side of the stairs. Sophie followed the light of her torch. Couldn't even see her at first. Just the pure blackness. Shadows dancing around them. Taunting them. Caressing them.

Sophie came up to the side of Tracy. She looked where Tracy was focussing the light from her phone. On the floor. Brought her light over to it too. In the middle of the floor—stone, she thought—there was something wet. Hard to see what in the artificial light from a couple of phones.

Sophie struggled, but crouched. The skin on the backs of her legs tore away from the denim it was stuck to, screaming pain up to her arse. She sucked air in through clenched teeth, but didn't say anything. She held her light closer. It was a material of some sort. Wet, and out of place in down there, where everything was so dry and still. Where a cloying must hung in the air. Like no one had been down there for a hundred years. She looked up at the camera.

But someone had.

Sophie used the edge of the phone to poke at it. It was soft. Sticky. Thin. She picked it up. Held it out. Oh Jesus. She tossed it aside.

"What?" Tracy asked.

"Fucking skin," she said. It was small, thin. Looked like the skin from a child, but she didn't say that. She didn't need to freak Maria out any more than she already was. "Let's just find a way out," she continued. Standing. She flashed her torch around. The basement seemed vast. Glanced back to the stairs. Maria was still there, waiting. She looked like she'd shit herself.

Who would blame her?

Sophie stepped over the skin, sitting in a coagulating pool of sticky blood. Strode into the darkness. Enough of this shit. She wanted out. *Now.*

She walked until she saw a wall. Twenty feet? Thirty. "Here," she said. "I've found the edge." She turned, expecting to see the light from Tracy's phone hanging somewhere in the gloom between her and the stairs, and Maria standing on the stairs, still luminescent from the light of the floor above.

There was nothing but blackness behind her.

"Fuck," she muttered. "Maria?" she called out. "Trace?"

The only reply she had was from the sound of her own breath. The beating of her heart, loud in her chest. The sound of her blood rushing around her body. And then the sound of another's breath. Something in the darkness.

"Hodder," she said quietly.

"Pretty," came the voice in the dark back towards her. Rasping. The Bound Man, once again.

"What do you want?"

"The same thing I always did."

"The warmth," she replied.

"Yes," he said. The word was elongated, like he was pleased with her understanding.

"Freedom."

"They are the same."

Sophie flashed the light around. There was the stone floor, she could see that, but nothing else. There was nothing. No walls. No ceiling. Nothing. It *had* to be an illusion. Like the rooms. Like before. The skin on her back needled her. The pain was real enough, though. "What does it mean?" she asked, quietly. "You have me now. You can answer."

CHAPTER 17

A rasping laugh. "Yes. I do. The flesh is my warmth. My freedom."

"Like when you killed the child."

"Like when I killed the child."

"Why?" Sophie was moving slowly in the darkness. Trying to find her way back towards where the stairs were. They must still be there. She just couldn't see them. The others had to be there, too.

"My son did not show you what I did to him after he was dead. He did not know the unbounding desire I had in life. One that burned me so deep."

"But you're dead now." She was still moving. Sure she was going in the right direction. "You don't need to do this anymore."

"Oh, but I do. The desire is no less. Perhaps it is more."

Sophie kept the light down on the floor so she didn't fall. Only flashing it up occasionally to try and see if she could find the stairs. She'd been moving for too long now. They weren't there. They weren't where they were supposed to be. She flashed the light up. Hodder blocked her way. Naked. Bound by wire, torn into his flash. Blood weeping from him. Maniacal grin. Blood stained teeth. She let out a little shriek. A small yelp of surprise, turning, running in the other direction.

She didn't know where she was going. She stopped. Which way were the stairs? Where was the wall? She turned, spun, looking around her, the torch flicking light all around and there was nothing but the stone floor.

Then there was him.

He was right next to her. "I have to be satisfied." He grabbed at her. Took both of her wrists in his hands. She dropped her phone. Heard it clatter to the floor, then she was plunged into darkness.

Blinded, Sophie screamed, kicking her legs out, connecting with nothing. With pulling at her wrists, she was lifted from the floor. Her toes slipping away from the stone as the vice grip Hodder had on her, dragged her into the air.

Agony ran through her as the skin on her back was pulled, cracking her wounds open. She felt the warmth of her blood as it trickled forth. "Fucker," she screamed. She called for help. But the others were gone.

As she kicked her legs she could feel the stone beneath her, she was moving. Behind her. She could see some light. It fingered her peripheral vision. Teasing her. But she couldn't see Hodder.

He was just *there*. Holding her.

A smell lifted into her nose. Something rancid. Horrid. Smelt like something had curled up and died some time ago.

Dragged through a doorway, Sophie was blinded by the light suddenly surrounding her. It burnt into her retinas. She closed them as they wept. Blinking. Hodder was there. He was holding her up by her wrists, an immense show of strength. Power.

He was grinning. Bloody. Ready.

He carried her into the room and she managed to open her eyes enough, look around, to see where she was. The room was tiled. Dirty. It looked like an old hospital operating room. He dragged her. She felt the cold hard touch of something as he pulled her over a table, a gurney, something. Held her down. He leaned over her, his blood drooling from the cuts in his skin, pale, clammy to the eye. It spit onto her, stringy, sticky, cum-like, as it dropped onto her clothes ... her skin ... her face. Onto her lips. He bound her arms with restraints like she was a patient on a mental ward. Tied to the bed. She screamed out. Spat into his face as he held it there, just inches from her own. He pulled back, running his fingers into the mucus, sliding it from his face to his fingers, and then dipping them into his mouth.

Tasting her.

His smile didn't waver as he reached down with the same fingers and ran them across her cheek. "So warm," he said.

Sophie kicked out her feet, trying to contact with him, but he stepped away from her, out of reach. Letting her see more of him, her eyes getting used to the light in the room now. He was naked. Hard. His cock bled like the rest of him. Wires digging deep into the flesh. Pushing the blood from his body, never ending. Leaving trails wherever he stood. Whatever he touched.

He touched himself. Like a fucking pornstar keeping themselves hard between takes. Fucking fluffing himself.

"Maria," she screamed. She was crying. Tears of fear. Harder to breathe, her nose blocked. Snot dribbling out onto her face. "*Tracy!*"

Hodder laughed. His voice breaking like a pubescent arsehole. "You cannot leave," he said, quiet.

Sophie looked around the room. Frantic. Something to help her escape. Anything. The tiles went from floor to ceiling. Across that too. Fluorescent lighting above, flickering every now and then. Grime laden everything. Like the room had been dormant for a millennia.

"Mine now," he said. Hodder stepped forward. "Like the others."

The smell of death in the room was overpowering the smell of iron from the blood. The ever-gushing blood. He stood over her. Held her foot down. Bracing that as well. Then the other. It didn't seem to matter what she did, how much she fought, he was stronger than her. Harder.

Unbreakable.

Hodder stepped away, again. Turning. There was a trolley behind him. She hadn't seen it before. She was *sure* it wasn't there before. She closed her eyes, tightly. There was no way she was going to beat him. He had … power.

The noise of him moving things on the trolley made her open her eyes again. She stared at him. His back as he faced away from her. He turned to face her. He had a pair of shears in his hand. He opened them. Closed them. Snapped them like a pair of garden shears.

"What are you going to do?" Sophie wept.

Hodder walked to her. Holding the shears up, pointing them at the ceiling. He leant over her, bringing his blood, gross, face close to hers. "The question really is *what am I* not *going to do to you?*"

Sophie could feel the puke inside her. It had settled at the back of her stomach, and was thinking about rising up, into her mouth. She concentrated on it. There was nothing she could do to remove herself from where she was now, so she would take her mind elsewhere.

Puke. Vomit. Seemed to be the best place for now.

Hodder brought the shears down and started to cut Maria's sweatshirt from her. He slid the blades around the material, starting at the front and cut upwards, towards her face. So careful not to touch her skin with the coldness of the blades.

CHAPTER 18

Hodder slowly cut her clothes off. Enjoying it. Sophie fought, but there was little point. She screamed. There was no one to hear. When he had her naked on the table, the rags that used to be her clothes discarded to the floor, he stood over her. The shears dropped to the dirty tiled floor. Of no more use. He ran his fingers from her hips up her torso, leaving behind a trail of cold blood, gooey on her skin.

Sophie shook. Uncontrollably. She was crying. Eyes closed. Not knowing what was coming next.

"Open your eyes," he said. "I desire you to watch."

She didn't. Sophie just wanted to puke. That wasn't rising either. She could taste it in her throat, but it wouldn't come out. She shook her head. No. She wasn't going to watch him do whatever it was that he was going to do to her. She wouldn't give him *that* satisfaction.

Hodder pushed his fingers against the skin above and below her eye and pushed it apart. Opening it. She looked around wildly. Desperate not to meet his stare. She didn't want to look. Shaking. Cold. Scared. He made this short chuckle under his breath. Let her go. Walked away. Sophie opened her eyes. He had returned to the trolley on the other side of the room. He prepared something, then came back to her. She closed her eyes before he could see she was watching him.

Afraid.

Alone.

Sophie stopped crying. It was like the tears weren't there anymore. Dried up. The fear was still twisting her gut though.

She could *feel* him standing over her.

He touched her face again. This time, when he pushed her eyes open, she immediately focussed on the needle that was there. An inch from her eye. A hooked needle, curled. Threaded. Hodder plucked her top eyelid from its place, resting on her eyeball, holding it out, away from her. The liquid, the moisture, drying up, stinging at her eye. She tried to blink. Close it. But he held it firmly. She could see him. His bloody finger holding her skin out. His shallow wheezing breathing cutting the silence.

She felt herself piss.

Couldn't stop herself. It just came out. She hadn't even thought about.

He realised. Chuckled to himself, again. Then stuck the needle into the skin of her eyelid. Sophie tried to move her head out the way, but he held her firm. The pain jabbed at her. It felt like he was squeezing her eyeballs, but all he touched was her skin. The needle went through, out the other side. Then he pushed it through Sophie's skin just below the brow. Through, out above it. Sewing the eyelid to the face. He zigzagged the stitch three times before breaking the thread with his fingernails. Then he did the same to the other eye.

Half blinded by the blood running into her eyes, darkening her vision, Sophie begged for the darkness to take her completely. She wanted it to go away. All of it. Perhaps even for death to take her. The air of the room took the moisture from her eyes, making them burn, as tears could no longer be created.

He grinned down at her. "Better," he said. She wasn't really listening.

He went from her again. Back to the trolley. What now? He was only there a second before returning. He held a knife. Big one. Hunting type. He held it above her face so she could get a long proper look at it. Taunting her with it. "My tastes are …" He looked down her body. "… strange." He rested the knife down on her stomach. She could feel the coldness of the blade on her skin. And Hodder started to caress her flesh. Touching her skin. Massaging her. She tried to move away from him, tried to curl up in a ball, but was bound too tight. He let his fingers roam her mound, sliding in between her legs, touching her cunt. His blood giving him the moisture he needed to rape her body with his fingers. Just a little. He grunted some sick, sadistic, satisfaction before withdrawing them.

This is it, she thought. *He's going to rape and kill me. Here. In this basement room. A room that's not even real.* She didn't think it was, anyway.

He tasted his fingers. Supped the blood from them. There was none of her taste there. She knew that much. But he seemed impressed with it, nonetheless. She so wanted to close her eyes and not watch.

Hodder picked up the knife.

Maybe he was going to kill her first? *That might not be such a bad thing*, she thought. She wanted to scratch her eyeballs, burning globes that they had become.

Hodder took the knife and drew the tip of the blade down her skin. Starting at her nipple. Across her breast. Down, she could feel it, on her ribs. To the side of her torso, away from where she could see. Then the searing pain came.

Starting as a burning, sharp scratch, the pain blossomed out, taking her breath. She sucked air in, too afraid of the feeling that might be caused by releasing it. She tried to close her eyes, sure it would help, but all she could do was stare into The Bound Man's face, tight with a grin as he moved the blade around the inside of her body.

He was careful to not cut away at anything on the inside. Working without looking, practiced as he was, he just increased the size of the hole the knife had made, until he pulled it out.

The expression on his face was a mix of serene, and happy. Joy with desire. His sexual appetites released to the fore. His wont plain. Arousal dripped from the tight edges of his lips. He finally looked down to the wound he'd made in her side. Taking his eyes from hers. Like lovers at the point of orgasm, the whole time.

Sophie could feel the blood coming from her. From the gash in her side. The spike of pain dulled to a hard throb, a bloom around the area, to the point that she could no longer feel the skin itself, numbed by the act. The fear? Who knew?

Hodder did. That was for sure. She could feel him teasing the slit in her skin with his fingers. Each touch a sear, a burn. He nodded some appreciation, muttering the word, *yes.*

He returned his look to her. Their eyes meeting once again, and then she felt him inside her. Roaming. Probing. He brought his hands up to her breasts and lay them on her skin, squeezing.

She could feel his hard cock pushing her insides about as his hips, squirming, caused the top half of his body—all she could see of him—to dance a slow Bolero. She could feel him, pushing his head against her intestines. She clenched as the movement caused her arsehole to want to give. And further, he moved. His blood mixing with hers inside her body. Their juices becoming a cocktail.

He moved harder. Faster.

Squeezed her tits like she was some cheap whore.

Sophie wanted to fight, pull away. Anything to stop this … monster from touching her. She screamed out. Staring into his eyes as they bled lust.

Then a warmth spread across her belly. Below the skin. Hodder shuddered, drawing to a stop. His lips parted, bloody, pink drool, gripping both the top and bottom lip, strung from them. A slight smile. His breathing hard, sharp, yet shallow, rasping.

He pulled himself from her.

Leaving the warmth behind.

Sophie felt her organs shift, back into position, undamaged apart from the introduction of his vile seed. Like he'd done this before, many, many, times. Allowed himself the luxury of keeping her as some rancid sex girl. Finishing without harming her flesh enough to kill her.

He unclenched his fingers. Released her skin. He picked up the knife from out of her sight again. "Warm," he muttered. He lifted the knife into her view, tilting it, trying to get the light to glint on the blade.

She stared at it, eyes of fire.

"But I won't keep you," he said. "There are others."

Sophie looked around, half expecting to see Maria and Tracy stood in the room too. But he meant that they were there in the house. They needed to be … disposed of … too. He slid the blade gently over her skin again. Clearly aroused by the threat. The way it stopped her breathing. The way she tore her stare from him as the blade took it. She could see his cock rising again from the flaccid, out of sight below the line of her stomach, popping up like a gopher from a hole.

"Oh, my." He whispered. Any other place, she wouldn't have been wrong thinking he was trying to be seductive. Here? No. He was turned on. Horny like a cunt, fucking teenage boy, confronted with the body of a real woman for the first time. The excitement of seeing her react to the blade was too much. He was ready to fuck her.

Again.

She looked from the blade to him. He was staring at the tip of the steel, dancing around her flesh. His other hand was on his cock. With each stroke forward, blood oozing from the cuts and slashes made by the metal bindings, cutting into him. He made a filthy, guttural sound, some deep disappointment. "But I can't," he said, all but a whisper.

He lifted the knife gently from her breast, and brought it swiftly to the skin under her rolled up chin, as she held it tight to her chest, watching him. Watching him torment her with the knife, pleasuring himself at the same time. A rasped sigh inwards, his grip tightened on the hilt of the knife.

CHAPTER 19

"Mumma." The voice of the Great Child filled the room as it tumbled through the door. "Mumma!" it wailed again.

Sophie looked from Hodder to the child and back again. "Help me," she screamed. "Help mumma."

The child lolled to the side of the table, to next to Hodder. It was unsteady on its feet, struggling to stay upright. First steps. The Great Child was taller than Hodder, oversized baby-fat making the thing twice his size across. It screamed, its pudgy massive face contorting into the face of a child who had lost its favourite toy. He pushed Hodder without skill or grace, two hands flat on his bare chest, slicking the child's hands with his blood. The weight of the baby carried through, and Hodder lost his footing, falling to the floor.

The lights went out.

Came back on.

Sophie was sure she moved when the lights were out. Hodder's hold broken for that instant. "Help me, Help Mumma," she shouted again.

The baby looked at her, massive baby tears in its eyes, on its fat cheeks. He turned to Hodder, lying at his feet, slipping as he struggled to get up, his mind concentrating on keeping control in the room. Keeping the room's mass intact.

The Great Child still had a massive cock, covered in baby hands all moving independently, reaching forward, grabbing at anything it could reach and pulling. Except it was flaccid now.

The child stamped on Hodder. He cried out, the sheer weight of the child hurting him, the distress enough to take his concentration.

The lights went out again.

Sophie moved. She was on the floor. There. There was her phone, the light still on. She picked it up.

Blinked.

Mother fucking blinked.

She shone the torch around.

The lights came back on. In the operating room. She was standing now. The phone in her hand. The illusion was breaking down. She reached down and felt her side, pain erupting through her. She staggered, steadying herself on the table she had been restrained on, only a moment ago. Blood drooled and dripped from it. Her blood, visible strings of cum floating in it. Slipping from the edge of the table and hanging like fresh pizza cheese. She felt vomit rise in her throat, but she swallowed it back. *Not now.*

The baby fell forwards, onto Hodder.

He disappeared beneath the flabby massive little thing. A scream.

Sophie could hear Hodder fighting. Shouting—rasping—for the child to get off him.

Darkness flooded her again as the room disappeared. She shone the phone around. Could see the light from the stairs. "Tracy?" she shouted.

"Soph?" came the response from the darkness. "I see you. This way. I've found a coal hatch."

Sophie took a single step forward. Realised there was no pain. She touched her side. No blood. She was naked, though. She stopped. Looked for Tracy in the darkness. Then to the light from the stairs. "You go," she called back. "I'm gonna burn this place down." She heard footfalls in the dark. A glance to The Giant Child ensured that it wasn't Hodder, still fighting for supremacy.

Tracy appeared in the darkness. She didn't even look at Hodder. The baby. Sophie assumed she couldn't see them. Oh well. "What the fuck?" she blurted. "We need to get the fuck out of here. Do you know what I just saw?" She stopped talking. Looked down Sophie. "You're naked again."

Sophie snapped her fingers at her. "Lighter," she demanded.

Tracy thrust her hand in her pocket "How did you know?" She pulled it out.

"Lucky guess." Sophie held her hand out for Tracy to pass it to her.

Tracy shook her head. "No way. I've always wanted to torch a haunted house." She looked over her shoulder. "Maria?" She continued without waiting for an answer. "Get the fucking coal hatch open. We'll be back." She turned, hurried back towards the stairs. "Come on then."

Sophie looked down at herself. Naked. Bloody. Her back stung, her legs raw. *Fuck it*, she thought. *Burn the fucker*.

She ran bare foot after Tracy.

CHAPTER 20

Sophie reached the bottom of the stairs. She saw the light from Maria's phone on the other side of the basement. She was doing something. Hopefully that was good. She turned up the stairs. Tracy was already at the top. She had pulled off her hoodie and tossed it to Sophie as she ran up the stairs behind her. "Try to keep hold of that one. It's my favourite." She flashed a smile at her.

"You okay?" Sophie pulled the hoodie over her bare skin. It stuck to her back, tacky with blood, but hung down enough that she *felt* dressed.

Tracy shrugged, wearing only a tank top now.

The two of them were in the hallway. Empty. No table in the middle of the floor. Nothing. "Damn it," Sophie muttered. She headed into the living room. The fire was out. Cold. Never lit. The furniture gone. The Bound Man and The Giant Child too busy to create anything with their minds. She looked around the room. Nothing but a radiator nestled below the window in the bay. The furnace must have been false, she thought to herself. She turned. The library. Burn the books?

She opened the door.

The room was empty. Of course it was. Not even a children's nursery now. "Fuck," she screamed.

"I know," Tracy said, hurrying out, back into the hallway. She went to the kitchen, clutching the lighter. Burst through the door, followed closely by Sophie. The table was gone. The fridge. Everything. As bare as the rest of the house.

"What?" Sophie asked.

"Here," she said. She went across the centre of the kitchen to the boiler on the wall. Old gas boiler. "Radiators in the other rooms, right?" She shot a wink at Sophie.

Sophie smiled. "Gotcha."

Tracy started wiggling taps and shit on the bottom of the radiator. "How do you turn this thing on?"

Sophie looked around the bare room. She pulled open one of the drawers, empty. But kept pulling. Pulled the old chipboard drawer from the kitchen cupboard, until she held the thing in her hand.

Tracy glanced to her, still twiddling knobs. "What are you doing?"

Sophie brought the drawer up, over her head and then slammed it down onto the tiled floor, on its corner. It smashed. Shattered. Bits of old chipboard flying everywhere.

Tracy let out a surprised *eep*.

Sophie bent down and pulled the metal drawer handle from the wood. About eight inches long. Concaved c-shaped. Iron, maybe. Tracy stared at her. She followed the two pipes from the blue and the red taps under the boiler. Water. Ignore those. Then levered the handle between the pipe that she was sure held gas, and the wall.

Then she yanked and twisted as hard as all the anger contained in her would allow.

The pipe popped off the boiler, and a hissing sound followed.

"Thank fucking shit," Tracy said. "The gas is still on."

Then the room was overtaken by the acrid smell of gas pluming out into it. Sophie covered her mouth with her hand and waved Tracy to follow as she left the room, out into the hallway. The two of them went to the top of the stairs to the basement.

Tracy thumbed the lighter, flicking fire out of it.

Sophie picked up Maria's backpack. She shrugged, holding it out towards the lighter. "All in a good cause," she said.

Tracy lit the thing up. It took like it was made of kindling. Fucking made in China, no doubt. She dropped it to the floor, burning. "Come on."

The two of them ran to the top of the stairs. Down. Into the darkness. Tracy turned the light on her phone to the stairs, allowing the two of them to see.

They got to the bottom of the stairs.

Then there was a *whump*. A sound like a car colliding with a brick wall, somewhere else in the house. Sophie ducked out of instinct, looking around in time to see a flash of light at the door at the top of the stairs, and the floor shook, the two women grabbing each other in an attempt to stay up right.

The house was burning.

Tracy looked around the room. The trap door leading out closed. "No," she whispered. She started towards the door, when a loud cracking sound cut through the air.

Sophie looked up. There was fire. She could see it between the floorboards. Raging above them. She ducked down, took Tracy's arm. "We need to go," she shouted over the roar of the fire.

Another splitting sound, and part of the ceiling—over where the kitchen was above it—crashed down to the floor.

"Where's Maria?" she shouted.

Tracy was looking around the basement. The fire providing more and more light as the room round them started to burn. Then, coming from the fire, The Bound Man came. Unrelenting. Unharmed by the fire. Just the binds. The blood, letting as always. He strode straight to the space between them and the trapdoor. Blocking their exit.

Tracy screamed. The first time she had seen Hodder like this.

He grinned a bloody grin, some self-satisfaction at the ending that involved him having the two of them. *Winning*.

Then The Great Child came. It came from the side of him, streaking from the darkness, still unwieldy on his feet. He grabbed Hodder, his cock grabbed Hodder, the two of them struggling. The thousand baby hands on its giant cock held Hodder's left hand, while its two chubby baby hands of adult size held his other arm. He screamed out in anguish. Hate. Fear. The two of them collapsing to the side.

The trapdoor behind them opened.

Maria.

She stuck her head down. Looked at the two fighting, then to Tracy and Sophie. "Come on," she shouted.

The baby pushed Hodder to the side of the three steps leading up to the trapdoor, the flames licking the ceiling around them.

More of the wood fell.

Parts of the rooms above dropping, flaming to the floor.

Sophie ran forward, pulling Tracy by the arm. She pushed her onto the stairs, and Maria grabbed her, pulling her out, into the cold night air.

"Mumma," the child cried, distracted for a second from the fight with Hodder. Hodder repaying the distraction, by slashing the baby's torso open with the blade he now held in his hand.

Angered, the baby turned back to him, just as the ceiling above them gave, and the burning wood crashed down onto them, taking them from Sophie's sight.

"Come on," screamed Tracy from just above her.

Sophie turned, ran up the stairs, and out, into the rain.

EPILOGUE

Sophie stood in the rain. The water trickled down the backs of her bare legs, cool on the welts, cuts, and sores. Washing the blood from her.

She looked back to the house. The three of them, stood in the field behind the house. Watching it burn. She could see the baby. He stood just beyond the trapdoor, the light of the fire behind him, silhouetting him in the blackness. He raised his chubby hand and gave a little baby wave.

Sophie waved back. Slowly. Sure, that neither of them could get out from the house. Trapped in there, in some eternal struggle. Father against son.

"What just happened?" Maria asked.

"Hodder killed his family," said Tracy slowly. "And a lot of others besides."

"Phone?" Sophie looked at Tracy.

She pulled it from her pocket, shook it at her. "Fire brigade?"

"Nah." Sophie took Tracy's phone and swiped the screen. Opened What's App. Dialled Will.

He answered. Looked confused. "Wow," he said. "That was some fucking fight you put up in there. Got it all on camera too. Look," he continued. "Nothing personal, right."

The three woman gathered around the screen so

he could see all of them. Shivering. Cold. Frightened. Hurt. "Will, darling," Sophie said. "You better run. Because we're gonna find you, and fuck you up."

About the Author

Ash is a British horror author. He resides in the south, in the Garden of England. He writes horror that is sometimes fantastical, sometimes grounded, but always deeply graphic, and black with humour.

Made in the USA
Monee, IL
22 September 2023